CITYSCAPES

A Collection of Short Stories

Janet Taliaferro

ISBN: 1546819789
ISBN 13: 9781546819783
Library of Congress Control Number: 2017911075
CreateSpace Independent Publishing Platform
North Charleston, South Carolina

Cover design by Pat Bickner

To Sarah

INTRODUCTION AND ACKNOWLEDGMENTS

The stories in *CityScapes* were written over a period of almost twenty-five years. I began writing them in the 1980s when visiting my two older children who were living in New York City, often staying with them in various apartments in Brooklyn, Astoria, and Manhattan. The impetus to tie the stories to New York came from my struggles to find an agent or a publisher during my early years as a writer. It seemed no one was interested in anything set outside New York.

However, I did include in this collection "Houses of Bondage," set in my home city during the 1930s and the Jim Crow era, because I thought it an important subject. All the other stories are connected, even tenuously, to New York.

On one of my trips to the city, I met with a fiction editor from *Redbook*. Their interest in two of my stories from an earlier collection that comprised my master's thesis was a real encouragement. Subsequently, the fiction department chose "Mrs. Parkhurst's Martini" for publication, only to have it pulled at the last minute by the senior editor. Nevertheless, I want to acknowledge the interest of *Redbook* as a major reason why I have continued to write. As a child of the Depression, I grew up on the fabulous short stories and novellas in *Redbook, McCall's,* and *Ladies' Home Journal.* In addition, Amazon and its subsidiary, CreateSpace, has made publication of books like this affordable for authors such as I, who are readable but not quite able to make it over the traditional publishing hurdle.

Just as important was the faculty in the writing program at the University of Central Oklahoma—especially Drs. Lynette Wert, Christopher Givan, and Clift' Warren; Professor Bill Gammel; and writers-in-residence John Bishop and Stewart O'Nan. Their guidance and critique have been invaluable.

Literary publications have been a welcome outlet. *New Plains Review* published several of my earlier short stories, and the beautiful *Northern Virginia Review,* edited by Dr. Dorothy U. Seyler, published both "The Last Civilized Act" and "North of South Carolina," honoring each with prizes.

In addition, I want to thank my author friends and readers, Dr. Seyler and Tara Woolpy, both of whom were kind enough to contribute comments for the cover of this book.

Not least, I want to thank my indefatigable editor Arnie Friedman, who not only corrected my geography of New York City as a native of the Bronx but also edited nearly everything I have written and knows the depth of my inability to spell or punctuate. And lastly, thank you to all my readers.

TABLE OF CONTENTS

THE LAST CIVILIZED ACT

L unch in Washington and dinner in New York—all in one day—would be perfect, Constance Steele thought, if only you didn't have to go through New Jersey.

She stared out the window of the Amtrak coach, thinking how much she hated the disorder of the right-of-way. Even nature conspired to create a mess, bunching piles of fall leaves in gullies and around trees. Scattered among them were the discards of habitation: a refrigerator, a sofa of indeterminate color, and a stove, its oven door ajar like the slack jaw of a skull.

This trip is a paradigm, she thought—one end of her life anchored in the legal career that had taken her to Washington for the day, and the other firmly attached to her husband, Graham, in New York. Gentle Graham, whose only passions were for her and for his books. Somewhere between the law and Graham was the truth. Truth was in her own body. The truth was that she was dying.

It was also her birthday, and Graham would be waiting to take her to dinner. Nausea tugged at her stomach, but she would not plead illness and deprive him of the pleasure of celebration.

The tunnel under the Hudson cut out what was left of a gray autumn sunset and made a mirror of the dark window. Constance examined her reflection as she stood to retrieve her worn briefcase from the overhead rack. The Chanel jacket, piped in black, disguised the fact that she was wearing the latest in medical paraphernalia, a miniature pump strapped to her waist that dripped poison into her liver upon the command of a silicon chip.

"The device," she called it and proudly explained its workings to the few close friends and family who inquired about the experimental treatment. To herself, she called it "the vise"; she hated the feeling of being at the mercy of modern technology and ignored the fact that it represented a last, desperate effort to stem the ravages of cells gone mad. At least it did not show. A judicious choice of clothing kept her silhouette unremarkable. Her hand smoothed the waist of the reflection. She did not look at her face. The train moved into the station, and the image disappeared, erased by dirty yellow lights.

In their glare stood Graham, a small man in a dark suit and dark hat with a British all-weather coat in the crook of his left arm and hands folded over the grip of a collapsible black umbrella. There must be only ten men in Manhattan who still wear a homburg, she thought, smiling at the ridiculous hat on his head. He reminded her of a Magritte painting. His clear gray eyes often allowed his thoughts to be seen as easily as a bird flitting about an open cage. Lately, the cage seemed to be draped.

Ready to offer assistance, he came toward her as she reached the door of the car. She wasn't too proud to take his arm and hand him the heavy briefcase. As they made their way into the terminal, she slipped her arms into a mauve silk raincoat.

"How was your day?" he asked. Concern pulled his eyebrows toward the bridge of his nose.

"Spectacular. I think we're going to win before the SEC," she said.

His expression did not change during her short recitation of the day's events. "But how do you feel?" he asked when she had finished.

"Oh, all right. Look, let's not talk about it. Okay?"

Graham didn't answer but turned his attention to hailing a taxi. They used to walk everywhere from their apartment just east of Central Park: to the grocery and meat market, the cleaners, the drug store, and out shopping. One lazy Sunday, they walked all the way to the Battery, just for exercise, but now he insisted they ride in cabs for even short distances.

He directed the cab to a restaurant, half a block off Washington Square. It was their favorite, an unpretentious Italian restaurant down a few steps from street level.

The sight of snowy linen and clean crystal, dark wood, and a minimum of red wallpaper pleased Constance. Ordinarily, she also anticipated the well-blended odor of tomatoes, garlic, and olive oil. Tonight, she fought a battle with her gorge instead.

Graham ordered carbonara, and she a plainly dressed angel hair, half of which she ate, along with a crusty roll. The wine was sour on her tongue.

Conversation ranged from news to sports, to weather, to the inane, and culminated in a near fight over whether their tickets to a performance at the Vivian Beaumont Theatre were for Friday or Saturday evening of the following week.

"Okay, Graham, okay," Constance said, "I give up. I was wrong."

He looked at her, uncertain.

"Not about the damned tickets, about it—me. We're acting like the proverbial elephant is in the room, and everyone's ignoring it. The elephant's real, and I can't ignore it another second. It's my birthday, and we both know it's probably the last one." The word "probably" echoed in her ears. Had she inserted that word for herself or for Graham? Short of a miracle, there was no "probably" about it.

"We don't know that. The doctor said…" he began.

"Graham, don't." She concentrated on pleating the stiff linen napkin against her thigh.

"But…"

"Graham! Screw the doctors. I'm dying." The forbidden words were said, and they hung like stale cigarette smoke between the couple. Constance felt a rush of relief followed by pangs of doubt. She stole a look at her husband.

His face sagged like the hem of an old gray sweater.

"Oh, darling," she said, "it's bad enough for me, but I *hate* it for you. God, to have to go through it all over again—it just kills me." She winced at the inappropriate cliché.

Graham seemed to rally. "That was different," he said.

"How? Hers was breast, and mine's liver. What's the difference?"

"Well," he hesitated, "Mother was sick so long."

"What makes you think I won't be?"

"There's no reason to discuss what we can't possibly know, Constance." His tone was dismissive, but his pale eyes slid away as if in fear.

The waiter brought coffee and cannoli, one with a single birthday candle, the dessert Graham had arranged in lieu of a cake.

Constance dutifully made a wish and blew out the candle.

"Did you make a wish?" Graham asked.

She nodded. She could see the curiosity in his eyes, but he probably had guessed what the wish was: God, please make it quick, and I don't want to hurt…at least for very long.

After a bite of cannoli, she said, "Promise me something, Graham."

He waited, wary.

"No extreme measures…and lots of drugs. If it can't be quick, have them make it painless, and if it can't be painless, for God's sake, make it quick. For both our sakes."

"I doubt if there is often much of a choice in that respect," he said. He looked helpless.

"But there might be. So promise."

"What are you asking me?"

She stared at him, and he returned her gaze without wavering.

"Constance, in all my life, I have tried never to do an uncivilized act. Please don't ask it of me at this point."

"Not uncivilized, Graham; just be kind." She hesitated and added, "I'm afraid."

For a moment, he did not respond. His fingers absently stacked and restacked the teaspoons, which lay unused by his plate. Constance could see the same faraway look in his gray eyes that shut her out when he was engrossed with his books.

"You are asking me to be your *kaishaku*," he said.

"My what?"

"In Japan, according to Shinto tradition, when someone commits suicide, ritual hara-kiri, there is always a second, the *kaishaku*, a nobleman who stands by with a sword, ready to cut off the head of the victim and end the pain. You're asking me to do that."

She felt a tiny prick of guilt. "I don't know. I guess so." She faltered.

"The problem is," Graham continued, "it sounds like a good idea now, sitting here at the table. I almost feel noble about being asked. About your confidence. But what happens when I have to act?"

"I don't know," she said, her voice hollow and forlorn. A moment ago, in the urgency of trying to make him understand her feelings, she had felt sure.

He looked away and signaled for the check. She stirred her cold coffee to hide the tears.

"Connie," he said and gently pulled her chin up so that she had to look at him, "I don't want to talk about any of this, because I'm scared. I don't know if I can take it—not just the end, but everything in between. I know it's selfish, but it's me I'm worried about. It was so long with Mother, and I guess I'm afraid I don't have what it takes to stand up to what's coming. You'll be fine. You'll bear up. But I feel...out of gas."

5

As the waiter approached with the bill, Constance excused herself and made her way casually between the tables to the ladies room. Her lack of haste was a deception, for the benefit of those around her and for herself. The moment she was in the bathroom, she went to one of the stalls and vomited everything she had eaten. She leaned with her hands against the wall until she felt settled enough to flush the toilet and turn to the lavatory. The girl from the coat check counter came in.

"You okay, Mrs. Steele?" she asked, a look of concern on her pretty face.

Constance nodded. "I'm fine."

"Okay," the girl said. "Just thought I'd check. I saw you come in, and you looked a little pale."

"Thanks," Constance said, "I appreciate your trouble."

The warm feeling of being cared for eased away some of the lingering nausea. When the girl had gone, Constance filled her palm twice with cold water and rinsed her mouth. Then she filled it twice again to get enough water to wash down two Dilaudid capsules. She had eaten them like candy all day. Smoothing her jacket, she could feel the plastic pack at her waist.

Graham looked at her suspiciously when she rejoined him. She raised her eyebrows in dismissal and shrugged into her coat. They left the restaurant and began to quarrel over transportation.

"Come on," she said, "the Fourth Street Station is right here and we can catch the F train."

"No, let me get a cab."

"Please, I want to walk. I love New York in the rain."

"But those gangs, or punks, or students, or whatever the stupid people are called sometimes ride the F. And there's all that business of transferring at Fifty-Third and the walk home."

"Gra-ham," she pleaded.

"Oh, all right. What the hell do I care if we get mugged or—" The words came in a rush of anger and then stopped abruptly, leaving him panting. His breath smeared almost invisible traces on the damp air.

"Killed?"

He didn't answer.

Constance put her arms around his waist. She could feel the smooth twill of the coat beneath her palms. The muscles of his back were tense columns flanking his spine.

"Oh God, I'm sorry," she said.

He put his free arm hard against her shoulders, pulling her against him. He spoke the words into her damp hair.

"Connie, a man is bound by the marriage oath to protect his wife. Right now, I just don't know how."

She looked up and smiled a radiant smile. Graham's reference once again to duty, honor, and contracts warmed her with the first real amusement she had felt all day.

He smiled in return, shook his head, and kissed her. Then he turned away from her embrace and guided her firmly toward the subway station. Their heels on the pavement tapped a companionable duet. He carried her briefcase in his left hand and held the umbrella open above her against the first real drops of rain.

The subway platform was neither crowded nor deserted. Constance stood close to Graham, his right hand protective against the small of her back. The lightly furled umbrella hung from his wrist, and she sometimes felt it tap against her buttocks.

Like a herd of gazelles, the knots of silent, waiting people raised heads in unison as a rush of teenage boys with the faces of men poured through the turnstiles onto the platform. Their voices were loud, shouting in the intimate assurance of a private patois.

Graham's worst fears, thought Constance. But the gang seemed more restless than threatening. Heedless, they roiled across the concrete, jostling the people on the platform, pushing them toward the tracks. Graham's hand pressed against Constance's back, making little grasping motions against the silk of her raincoat, as though to keep her from falling into the pit. They were pushed to the steel edge of the platform. Still the crowd pressed forward. Someone bumped roughly against her elbow, her shoulder. She heard the thud of the briefcase as Graham dropped it and clutched at her with both hands. Other, younger hands grasped at her body, arms, hair, and thighs. She felt the slick fabric that encased her slip away from the pressure of fingers. She was falling; damp gravel and bits of waste paper, steel rails, and torn Styrofoam rushed at her. Excruciating pain in her hip pierced the shield of Dilaudid. She moaned, her mouth wide open. She tried to rise, to move away from the rail. Pain and the rasp of grinding bone prevented her from doing more than moving her right arm and her head. Then, the pain seemed to drain away into a great lethargy. Only her arm and her mind had energy or volition.

A sea of white eyes, round with surprise, looked down at her. A young man paused in the act of climbing down from the platform, one long leg over the steel edge, a white sneaker almost touching the dirty gravel. He stared as she stretched her hand toward the third rail, her fingers barely missing the lethal electrified metal.

Graham saw the movement, too, his sad face a pale, almost featureless oval below the somber hat.

Constance tried to speak but no sound came. "Help me." She mouthed the words to Graham. With a barely perceptible movement, he flicked the half-open umbrella from his wrist. It made a graceful arc and fell just within her reach.

CENTRAL PARK SOUTH

"There will be four of us."

"Follow me, madam."

Helen Battaley followed the maître d'hôtel from the door of the Edwardian Room of the Plaza Hotel to a table close to one of the windows looking out on Central Park. She had not been in the old hotel in years. She glanced around at the new decor and sniffed the air, not so much to test it for odors of food but to register tacit disapproval of what she saw. She missed the jewel tones of the English chintz. The pale walls and ceiling above and the pale carpet below, coupled with the subtle blues and roses of the upholstery, gave her the impression of a world suspended, all activity taking place languidly between two voids. She was suffering from a slight eye infection. Without her contact lenses—God forbid she would wear her outdated glasses—her myopic state gave a view of the world as if painted by Monet and, in this case, a slight sense of vertigo as she walked toward the table. She sat down in the chair facing the window. The familiar scene of yellow taxis, trees, horse-drawn carriages waiting for tourists, and rain-slick streets gave her a sense that the world still operated in the realm of the familiar.

Stupid, she thought, having almost white carpet in a restaurant. Surely even New York waiters spill occasionally. Or Midwest tourists drop food.

"May I bring you something to drink, madam?"

Obsequious pip-squeak, she thought. "I'll have a Manhattan, straight up," she said imperiously. Helen rarely drank, particularly at noon, but today she was excited about being in Manhattan, so she thought it only proper to celebrate the place with its own drink.

As a young married woman, she had lived just across the river in New Jersey and visited New York often. Although she missed the advantages of the city, she was glad to move, twenty years ago, from what she considered a middle-class environment of struggling young executives-in-training, to affluent Hillsboro outside San Francisco. The West Coast suited her, and with no family in the East, she simply never went back to visit, losing contact with everyone she had known with the exception of Edith, who soon would join her for this lunch.

In truth, Edith was the one who faithfully sent the Christmas cards with photocopied letters describing the past year's activity in the Kelly family. Helen always sent elegant cards the day before Christmas, but only to those people who had been kind enough to mail greetings to her. More formal cards to Harold's business associates and their social friends in San Francisco were mailed weeks earlier from the office.

Originally, each couple's daughter had maintained the contact. The families lived next door to each other. Barbara Battaley and Megan Kelly, six months apart in age, were friends from the time they could toddle. When Barbara moved, just before the beginning of third grade, the girls were devastated. They talked by phone and kept up a slowly dying correspondence until they were teenagers. Their separate ways took Barbara to Stanford and Tufts. Megan had gone to Columbia and then Cranbrook, in Michigan, for an advanced degree in art.

Soon after Barbara graduated, she found a job with an arbitrage house in New York. In a moment of loneliness, she had called her old neighbor and found that Megan was living in the city. They renewed their friendship, found an apartment to share, and began to make an assorted and interesting group of friends. And now, for Helen, came the exciting part. Obviously, some young men of the group had caught the girls' interest. There were hints of falling in love in Barbara's letters home. She wasn't terribly direct, but Helen could read between the lines.

Finally, there was a letter that said she was wearing a ring and that Megan also had received one. Helen was smiling to herself when she saw Edith, following the maître d' across the restaurant.

"Helen."

"Edith. You haven't changed a day," Helen said, adding to herself, "simply aged, my dear, and not well." Her shrewd eyes took in Edith's thinness, the lines around her eyes and serious mouth.

She was always so serious, Helen thought, really mousy, and she's still wearing those East Coast preppy clothes, almost no makeup, and her own gray hair! Surely Megan had acquired some style in art school; otherwise, Helen wondered, how had she ever caught a man?

Edith ordered a glass of Chablis, and Helen, feeling daring, asked for a second Manhattan.

"I feel like celebrating," she said to Edith.

"You do?" she said with a bewildered look.

"Of course, I'm so happy for the girls. Isn't it just amazing that after all these years they got together here in New York and now this?"

Edith just nodded and took a sip of wine.

Edith's husband, Tim, had died three years before, and Helen assumed Edith must still be in mourning. "Tell me about yourself, Edith, and I'm so sorry about Tim."

With something of a look of relief, Edith began in her soft voice to spin out what was to Helen an incredibly boring tale of domesticity, capped by a recitation of Tim's final weeks. No wonder she's in the dumps, thought Helen, she's never done anything to keep her mind fresh. She raised one kid and catered to her husband.

When it was her turn to catch up on the past twenty years, Helen tried to keep the tone of triumph and self-satisfaction she felt out of her voice. Harold, her husband, was now CFO of a large West Coast company. She was involved, not just as a corporate wife, but in many civic activities. She was in the midst of talking about what she did for the M. H. deYoung Memorial Museum, when a small-boned young woman, dressed like a cross between a street person and Annie Hall, walked directly to their table. Megan kissed her mother, shook raindrops from her dark beret, and stuffed it into an enormous shoulder bag. She draped her long army surplus coat over the back of a chair, revealing a slight figure in a flowing skirt and shirt belted at the waist, long auburn hair, and amazing lapis lazuli eyes.

Helen's cool glance took in the only jewelry Megan wore, over-sized earrings, in execrable taste, according to Helen's opinion, and a circlet of rubies on her left hand. Helen assumed this was what passed for an engagement ring in Greenwich Village.

"It's nice to see you again, Aunt Helen," Megan said, reverting to the nomenclature the girls had used as children. She did have a charming smile, Helen had to concede.

"So, Megan, you're an artist," Helen said. "Tell me about your job."

"There's not much to tell, I'm afraid. I would love to do nothing but live in a loft and paint, but I'm working for a design firm here. They do all sorts of space planning on contract for large companies, which is what I do. It's interesting and it pays well, better than the proverbial starving artist."

"She's worked on two presidential libraries and additions to two major art galleries," Edith said.

"How interesting." Helen smiled. "I was just telling your mother about what was going on at the deYoung Museum." She continued her conversation as though there had never been an interruption, pausing only when she saw Barbara approaching the table.

My gorgeous daughter, she thought, and so chic, compared to Megan. Helen watched Barbara's long hair, the color of a sable coat, ripple against the shoulders of her severe black pant suit in a wake created by her purposeful, hasty stride.

"Hi, everybody. Sorry to keep you waiting. It's been one of those up and down mornings on the market." Her smile was radiant.

Well, it must be the fashion, Helen thought, noting the circlet on Barbara's hand, identical to Megan's but with sapphires as blue as her eyes.

"So, Mom, are you fine? I'm so glad you wanted to come to New York and visit. And how's Dad?" Barbara rushed into conversation as soon as she had ordered a Perrier and lime for herself and for Megan.

"He's fine; so am I, and I don't care about any of that. Now that everyone's here, I want to hear all about your love life," Helen said.

Megan looked embarrassed. Edith looked at her plate.

"You do?" said Barbara.

"Of course," said Helen, "you're both in love, and I want to hear every detail of these young men who have captured your hearts." Helen realized her enthusiasm made her words sound like a Harlequin romance.

"Mom, didn't you understand my letter? We are in love," Barbara paused, "but with each other."

Helen felt her face grow as cold and pale as the decor. The sense of vertigo returned, and not even the postcard scene of Central Park South looked familiar.

BY THE TIME I GET TO PHOENIX

**WANTED TO BUY: Mercedes
300SL-Gullwing. For further
information, call 516-5...**

Carmine DeSilva's coffee cup covered the rest of the phone number, but the Long Island area code caught his attention. He stared at the newspaper.

Reading the want ads had become a habit with him. It prolonged the morning ritual of silence, the only time, he thought, Angela ever was silent. At least she let him read his newspaper in peace.

He glanced at her furtively, hoping to avoid her attention. She continued to gaze catatonically at the kitchen window. He knew she could not see out. Two tiers of frilled curtains, faded and limp with age, covered the windows. Beyond the dingy glass was only the gloom of Thirty-Sixth Street.

Angela was smoking her third cigarette and drinking her second cup of coffee. Breakfast would consist of two more of each. The blue smoke from the end of the Marlboro dangling from her lip twined with the muddy clouds exhaled from her nose. Her face was fleshy below the pouty mouth. Carmine remembered with an inner sigh what the slender girl had looked like. He had thought the blond hair was natural.

Carmine looked again at the want ad and moved his coffee cup to hide everything but the words "wanted to." His mind was on the tarpaulin-covered shape that occupied the garage of the house. Their own 1979 Chevy always sat in the driveway between the closed garage door and the chain-link fence that surrounded the front yard.

The garage was opened four times a year. On good days in the spring and the fall, Carmine busied himself with seeing to the maintenance of the treasure that he drove only once every three months, just as his father had done.

Treasure. That was what his father had called the Mercedes. "My treasure chest, boy, and don't you sell it!"

His father, Geno DeSilva, had lived with them for seventeen years. Angela and the old man had fought over everything. She blamed their childlessness on him, claiming that if she had not had to worry with Geno, she would not be nervous and would be able to conceive. She never stayed with one doctor long enough to find out what the real problem was. Carmine wondered if it wasn't his fault. Perhaps he was sterile. But then, he told himself, he never had checked to find the truth, either.

"The creamer," said Angela.

"Huh?" mumbled Carmine.

"When you're at the store," she said. "You always forget the creamer."

Carmine stood and moved his coffee cup off the newspaper. The tabletop was cold gray laminate. He hated the design on the table, a maze of tiny figures overlapping. They looked like miniature boomerangs to him. The thought of so many objects always returning to their starting points depressed him. He shivered.

"You through with the funnies?" he asked.

Angela nodded, the cigarette glowed, and she bared her teeth, exhaling a cloud of smoke. Carmine found himself holding his breath against the acrid odor. He gathered the paper up with as deliberate a motion as he could affect and carried it and the cup to the sink. He washed his cup, his cereal bowl, and the filter apparatus for the coffeemaker. He would wash the pot when he came home from his twice-weekly trip to the grocery.

He tore the notice about the car from the newspaper and put the rest of it in the garbage sack. Angela glanced away from the window.

"Just an ad about a tire sale," he said, and he thought his voice sounded apologetic.

"Got the list?" was her only reply.

"Yes."

"Put creamer on it."

"It's on," he said and picked up the lined yellow slip from the counter.

"Check. You always forget creamer," she said as he made his way toward the hall closet for his old sweater. It never seemed to keep him warm these days.

At two that afternoon, Carmine walked along Thirty-Sixth Street, his lean frame immaculate in a starched white shirt, black trousers, and well-polished black shoes, with a formal bow tie at his throat. Carmine smoothed back his thinning, still dark hair with the palms of both hands and then smoothed his cheeks. His hands smelled pleasantly of aftershave.

It was his habit to say a prayer or two each day on his way to work, an old habit from school days when his mother would say, "Carmine, if you can't go to mass, you can always say a prayer. Practice on your way to school. Say a prayer; say two."

He and Angela hadn't been to mass in years, not since his father died. Angela hated to take the bus to get to the church, and parking around the building became increasingly difficult. They had watched the neighborhood change from a predominantly Roman Catholic, Italian community to one that was almost entirely Greek Orthodox. LaBella, the restaurant where he had worked as dishwasher, busboy, and finally waiter, was still on Atlantic Avenue, but ten years ago, at Angela's insistence, he had gone to work for Pete Stavros at the Neptune, a larger and busier establishment. His father had never forgiven him for "abandoning his own people," but Angela was happy with the increased income.

In appearance, the neighborhood hadn't changed all that much. It was just grayer and shabbier. Rows of attached houses with single garages, most of them faced with man-made stone of a doubtful color or with pale asbestos siding, stood behind fenced front yards. Links of aluminum chain separated the sidewalk from the plots of shabby grass. Gates were padlocked across short concrete driveways.

The houses reminded him of the miles of gray granite headstones in St. John's Cemetery along the Central Expressway. One day, he would move from his gray slab of a house with its small plot of ground to a granite slab of a grave close to his parents.

One headstone for another, he thought.

Carmine let his thoughts drift to the one time he and Angela had taken a trip. They had gone to California to visit a cousin of hers. They had driven the Chevy when it was not new, but a "recently purchased formerly owned automobile."

Angela had been appalled at the long drive, the immense distance between the two coasts, but he had been endlessly fascinated by the changing landscape, marveling at the broad sweep of the continent.

On the way back, they had gone through Phoenix. He often remembered the wide vistas, the clean look of the desert, and the giant saguaro cacti that grew between Tucson and Phoenix. And it was warm.

On impulse, he had suggested that they look at one of the retirement communities in Arizona. Angela hooted at the idea, but for once in his life, he argued her to a standstill. She sat in the car, using the partially folded map as a fan, while he toured one of the facilities.

"I don't want to live in no Sun City, and I don't ever want to talk about it again," she said when he came back to the car.

He remembered how he had stood there, unable to say anything. He had loved the feel of the sun on his back and the top of his head.

Now Carmine looked up at the iron-gray clouds that seemed to press down on the Triborough Bridge. He sighed and walked the last chilly block to the Neptune.

Pete Stavros stood in the kitchen talking to the cook when Carmine made his way to the alcove where the waiters had a cubbyhole for their coats. He hung his sweater carefully on the same hook from which he took his gold waiter's jacket. Carmine slipped into it with the same deliberation he used in all of his movements. Then he slowly took the clipping from this morning's paper from his pocket.

Pete turned and started for his office area behind the kitchen.

"Pete," Carmine said, "Got a minute?"

"Sure. One." Pete was always in a hurry. His shoulders rolled with his bouncing gait. Built like a welterweight, he always looked as though he was ready for a bout.

"What do you suppose a gull-wing 1954 Mercedes would be worth?"

"Jeez, Carmine, you been in my till?"

Carmine looked confused. Pete laughed.

"You thinkin' about buyin' one? Tips must be better than I thought."

This time Carmine laughed too, delighted. "Get outta here!" he said. "Pete, I never told you. My dad had one. Left it to me, along with the house that Angela and me live in."

Pete's black eyes were round as buttons. "You kiddin'?" Business always got his full attention. He leaned an elbow against the edge of the counter next to Carmine where the newspaper ad lay.

Carmine handed the ad to Pete. "Waddaya think it's worth?"

Pete scanned the ad and then said, "Let's find out." He picked up the scrap of paper in one hand, took the sleeve of Carmine's coat in the other, and pulled him into the office. "Want me to call?" Pete said.

"Would you?" Carmine asked, relieved.

Pete was already dialing, a cool look of detachment and cunning on his face.

The phone answered, and he asked for a Mr. Kolliopolis. After a pause, Pete introduced himself in a crisp, business voice. "Could you give me an idea of the resale price of a '54 Mercedes 300SL gullwing?" He listened and then put the mouthpiece against his shoulder. "How many miles?"

"Twenty-eight t'ousand," said Carmine.

"Twenty-eight." There was a pause. "No, honest to God. I'm askin' for a client, and this guy is as honest as the day is long, so help me. Yeah. It was his dad's car."

"His treasure chest," Carmine said.

Again Pete covered the mouthpiece. "He wants some background. Where was it driven and stuff like that, and what color is it?"

"Gray," Carmine said. "We took it on the road four times a year. Spring and fall, we went up the Hudson, far as Poughkeepsie. Winters and spring, Dad liked to drive out to Montauk."

Carmine was overwhelmed by a nervous desire to talk. "Dad had that garage down off Atlantic. He fixed a door handle on the car for a friend of Uncle Franco's. Uncle Franco's a lawyer. And the guy never came back. Finally Franco tells Dad that the guy's not coming back so he can just keep the car—even got the title put in Dad's name."

19

Pete relayed only the pertinent part of the information, nodding impatiently at Carmine but listening to Kolliopolis. He whistled through his teeth and said, "Holy Toledo. Okay, and I appreciate your time."

He slapped the phone onto its base. "How does two hundred sixty-five t'ousand bucks hit you?"

Carmine stared at him.

Pete's eyes were shining like those of a child who had been read a fairy tale. "Jeez, what a piece of luck," he breathed. He snatched up the phone again, dialing.

"Ah, yes." Pete's voice was suave. "Ah, I'm calling as to the ad placed in the paper regarding the purchase of a 1954 Mercedes 300SL...uh huh...mmm. I'm calling for a client, missus."

Carmine suddenly had a sinking feeling. Would Pete expect a cut? He was ashamed of his own greed.

"Right. Yeah." Pete was making faces into the telephone mouthpiece. "Thank you, missus. I certainly appreciate your help." He slapped the phone down again.

"Now, Carmine, here's the deal. The guy's a lawyer, big Wall Street firm. The missus said call him at home, late." He shoved the scrap of newsprint back at Carmine and was out the office door.

"Thanks, Pete," Carmine said.

Later in the evening, Carmine found himself with a slow time at his tables. He dialed the Long Island number and noticed that his bony fingers were trembling so that he could barely find the holes on the old rotary dial wall phone in the kitchen.

A man answered. Carmine introduced himself and asked if the gentleman had placed the ad.

"Yes," was the brief reply.

Carmine told him about the car.

"Of course, I would have to see it." The comment was cool.

"Oh sure. Anytime."

"And what are you asking for it, Mr. DeSilva?"

Carmine's mouth went dry, "Well...uh...well, I'm told its worth about...uh." Carmine swallowed, his gullet in spasm. He cleared his throat and rasped, "Two hundred sixty-five t'ousand." He felt a rush of blood to his face, but at least he had gotten the words out.

"Two hundred sixty-five thousand." There was a pause. "When could you bring it out?"

Carmine thought he was going to faint. He realized he had been holding his breath. "Any time," he said, "Well, when it's convenient. Well, I work nights, but that don't matter, whenever you want."

They settled on the following Saturday, exchanged names and addresses, and T. Howard Sandford bid Carmine DeSilva a rather cold good-bye.

The house was quiet when Carmine came home from work. Angela was asleep. Often, she was awake, watching television. She loved late-night television.

Carmine went to the garage door. The tarpaulin-covered shape took up most of the space. Carmine lifted the canvas away from the near side of the automobile and carefully jackknifed himself through the open window. The small garage did not allow him to enter through the wing-like doors, but Carmine was used to this sort of entrance and exit.

For a moment, he relaxed against the leather seats, the feeling of comfort and luxury seeping into his tired muscles. Angela may not have understood his father's affinity for this lovely machine, but he did.

At last, he opened the glove compartment and switched on the map light. Somewhat dim, he noted. The autumn drive was overdue and the battery needed a workout.

He removed the pseudo-leather envelope that he knew contained the car title, although he had never looked inside it. His father's angular handwriting had signed it and made the ownership over to Carmine. Also inside the envelope was a letter addressed to him. Carmine's hands shook as he tore the flap open. Inside was a letter in his father's crabbed hand. There was no salutation.

So she finally talked you into selling your inheritance. I just hope to God it's not because she wants to buy new furniture or some damfool thing like that. If it is, and you're smart, you'll wait until you are ready to retire. Then take the money if you want to, but for the Lord's sake, get it in cash. Nobody but crooks, even high class ones, ever buy this kind of car.

There was no signature, either.

On Saturday morning, as Carmine cleared away the breakfast dishes, he said, "I'm going to take the car out to Long Island. You want to go?"

Angela looked incredulous, the cigarette halfway to her full lips. "You kiddin'? The Jets is playing."

"It's a nice day, and I need to take the car out."

"So take the hunk of junk. God, you and your old man. Hang on to that thing, takin' up room. Fer what?"

For about two hundred sixty-five t'ousand dollars, thought Carmine, but he held his tongue.

"Just thought you might like to get out," he said.

"Go on," she said. "With the Jets playin'?"

Later, as he backed carefully out of the garage, she stood, still in her bathrobe, watching him. Her elbow was cocked, and she held a cigarette between the third and fourth fingers. The blond hair was still in pink plastic curlers.

Carmine gave a sigh of relief. He had been afraid up until the last moment she would change her mind. For now, this was his secret.

The address was in the old part of Garden City. The long green lawns and generous shingled houses bespoke comfort and settled money. Mostly, it was a façade; Manhattan's lucky and hard-working entrepreneurs owned the majority of the turn-of-the-century homes. These men, now reaching fifty, were not born to wealth but, with the assistance of good schools and a rising economy, had made fortunes.

Carmine rang the bell next to the red-painted door. A small roof, supported by wooden columns, covered the porch. T. Howard Sandford opened the door himself. He wore golf slacks and an expensive polo shirt of kelly green. The topsiders would be exchanged for golf shoes when he met his foursome at two thirty. The salt and pepper hair was carefully trimmed, the face smooth despite hours on the links.

"Mr. DeSilva?" he said and held out a hand.

Carmine was not surprised at the firm grip.

"Well, let's take a look," Sandford said, approaching the car with purpose.

Carefully dusted, the Mercedes's gray paint gleamed. Sandford opened both doors, and the automobile looked poised for flight, its long hood and slanted vents making it appear already in motion.

Sandford sat behind the wheel and ran his hand over the flawless leather, worn only slightly on the cording.

"Go on," Carmine said, "Take it for a spin."

For one moment, the wealthy lawyer looked like a small boy and then quickly reassumed his professional attitude. "Well, of course I will want to drive it, and I want my mechanic to look at it. In fact, I asked him if we could bring it by his house. He's right here in Garden City. I was sure you would understand my caution."

"Sure, go right ahead," Carmine said.

"Do you want to ride along?" Sandford asked.

"No, I know you ain't goin' no place," Carmine smiled.

Sandford hesitated. He seemed eager not to have Carmine along as he tried out the car but was undecided.

"Well, Mr. DeSilva, I can hardly leave you on the curb. Let me take you in and introduce you to my wife."

The next forty minutes were excruciating for both Carmine and Lelia Sandford, but to Carmine, it was worth it to see the joy on Sandford's face when he returned.

"You and your father have taken excellent care of that automobile, Mr. DeSilva," he said. "I must admit, I didn't really believe you when I talked to you on the phone, but my man says it is in A-number one shape. I think maybe we have a deal."

Carmine didn't know what "maybe" meant. He held his breath.

"I didn't want to pay more than two hundred thousand for one," Sandford said.

"The books says two sixty-five," said Carmine.

Lelia Sandford excused herself.

"Two twenty-five," said Sandford.

"Two fifty." Carmine was surprised at the note of finality in his own voice.

"Done deal," said Sandford and held out his hand.

"Just one thing," said Carmine.

Sandford dropped his hand suspiciously.

"Could I have it in cash?" said Carmine.

"Cash? Good God, man."

Carmine could see the deep mistrust in the man's clear gray eyes.

"Well, you see," sputtered Carmine, "it was my dad's wish. He wasn't very trusting, and he left me this letter with the car. Oh, no offense, Mr. Sandford, I'm sure you're honest, but…"

Carmine ran out of argument, and Sandford was still stunned.

"What about a cashier's check?"

"Cash."

"Look here, man. I don't want to carry two hundred and fifty thousand dollars around this city in cash, and neither do you. Take a cashier's check."

Carmine was adamant at first, but the problem of safety bothered him, too. They finally agreed on a cashier's check made out to Carmine for 150,000 dollars and 100,000 in cash, to be delivered the following Saturday morning.

The two men shook hands and Carmine settled into the car, driving it back to Astoria with utmost care.

"I've sold the car." Carmine didn't break the news until breakfast on Saturday.

"Wha-a-at? You sold the hunk of junk? Get outa here. That'll be the day."

"And I gotta deliver it by noon. You'll have to drive the Chevy, Angela."

"It's rainin', for God's sake. And there's a series game today," she whined.

"Get dressed, Angela. We gotta go to Garden City."

"Ah, fer Chrissake," she said. "And what did you get for it? Nothin', I'll bet."

Carmine's answer stunned her to silence. She stubbed out the cigarette. "You lyin' to me, Carmine DeSilva?"

Carmine began to clear the table.

If Carmine's first visit with Lelia Sandford had been embarrassing, Angela managed to mortify him even more. Angela would not relinquish her worn gray tweed coat, and managed to spill some of the cola her uneasy hostess offered. The drink spilled again when Angela made an unceremonious grab for the cashier's check, snatching it from Carmine's grasp.

The two men finished their business, Carmine putting the stacks of green bills away in an old zippered canvas tote bag he had brought for that purpose. He hung onto it, ignoring Angela's glare.

Sandford could not resist one piece of lawyerly advice. "Now look, here," he said, "It's none of my business, but this is going to put you right up in the top bracket this year. Don't forget the IRS is looking over your shoulder."

Carmine had already discussed this with Franco. "'Bout eighty-fi' t'ousand," he said, wagging his head in the way he thought businessmen did.

Sandford clapped him on the shoulder and walked the couple to the battered Chevy.

"Going to get a new car?" he laughed.

"And then some," Carmine answered. "Maybe we'll even retire and move to Florida or someplace."

Awe had curbed Angela's tongue at the Sandfords, but the ride home loosened it. She was ecstatic. The purse with the cashier's check was pressed to her bosom.

Carmine stole a look at her face. She was happier than he had seen her in years. She chattered on and on about the house and the furniture and the carpets and what they would buy. She made it clear that her plans stretched only so far as the Astoria house. Carmine ignored her, aware of a deepening depression. He was surprised that he felt the loss of the automobile. Felt the loss, and still nothing seemed to have changed. Not even Angela's usual complaint when, halfway down the Long Island Expressway, she said, "Carmine, you gotta stop. I gotta go to the bathroom."

He obediently found an exit and headed for the nearest gas station. He pulled the car to the side near the restrooms, and she fled to one, clutching her purse.

Carmine watched the traffic make its way on and off the expressway. He didn't want to go to work. He didn't want to go home. He wished Angela would even talk about moving out of Queens, somewhere warm. They could do it now: sell the house, trade cars, and even after taxes have plenty to invest for their old age. They had insurance, and it was paid up.

The bus from Manhattan snaked off the ramp and stopped across the street at a bus stop. The stop for the on ramp was twenty yards from where Carmine sat. The inbound bus was a block away, stopped in traffic.

Carmine opened the car door. His knee brushed the keys in the ignition, setting off a tinkling, like wind chimes. Automatically, he reached for the tote bag.

His body moved without volition, one foot in front of the other toward the bus stop. The bus was approaching; he could hear the hiss of the air brakes. He felt in his pocket for change. His entire body was numb.

Thoughts swirled thorough his head. How did people disappear? They did it all the time. Got away with it. How did you get a social security card? Open a bank account? Were the bills he carried traceable? Would anyone bother? What about Angela? She had the check, and they had a joint account. The house was in both of their names. She had the car. She had Uncle Franco. She had her cigarettes and her bladder and her mouth.

He boarded the bus, watching the car covertly as he walked down the aisle to an empty seat. Angela emerged from the restroom and settled into her side of the car, staring straight ahead as if waiting for him to come out of the men's room. She was pouting.

Carmine settled into the seat as the doors whooshed closed and the bus moved onto the expressway on its way to Manhattan, on its way to the bus station, on its way to freedom.

A sense of peace settled over Carmine, and he began humming strains from an old Glen Campbell song.

MRS. PARKHURST'S MARTINI

Margaret Parkhurst hesitated a moment as she put her hand on the polished doorplate. She smiled to herself. Thank God it was Friday. And thank God for Barney's Bar. She glanced through the beveled glass pane. The interior of the bar, lit by skylights, sparkled with brass fittings and glass stemware against a background of tan leather, blond oak, and the forest green of hanging plants.

The bevel of the glass vertically bisected the scene. Barney's figure became two, then one, and then two again as he moved in front of the mirrored back bar.

Margaret walked in and sat at the deserted bar. She leaned over the counter and smiled at Barney.

"Good afternoon, Mrs. Parkhurst."

"Good afternoon, Barney, and since it's Friday, I think I'll have my martini—on the rocks and with an olive, please."

She watched as he skillfully measured the colorless liquids and poured them quickly over the cracked ice. Barney always served martinis in a stemmed balloon glass. Margaret knew they really didn't taste any better served that way, but the elegance appealed to her.

Barney put two drinks in front of her. It was Friday afternoon happy hour.

Margaret breathed in the aroma of juniper, flavored with just a hint of vinegar from the olive speared by a yellow plastic sword.

She once heard someone describe a martini as the color of moonlight. She lifted the glass and took a sip of the slightly opalescent liquid. The drink was cold and astringent on her tongue. She sighed a little in relief and pleasure and studied her lone reflection in the glass behind the bar. She looked with satisfaction at herself. She was slender and still young looking at forty-one. Her good banker's gray suit was well cut. Her jewelry was simple and expensive: earrings and necklace from Bulgari and a hand-wrought gold wedding band on her left hand. Her dark hair, freshly cut, fell in feathery waves away from her temples.

She took a long swallow from her glass and enjoyed the pleasant burn as the martini settled into a warm pool in her stomach. Whatever tensions she had brought with her from the office dissolved like aspic on a warm day. Her worries might still be with her, but they could not hold their shape in such warmth.

"Hello, lady."

Margaret looked up again at the glass to see her friend Peggy whispering in her left ear.

"Hi, there. Come sit down, and you can have my other martini."

"Love to," Peggy said in a throaty voice.

The two women were so similar they could have been mistaken for sisters—but they were not.

"Where's handsome, debonair, untrustworthy John?" Peggy asked.

"Still at his office. He had some sort of important meeting. He'll meet me at the apartment around eight," Margaret said.

"I suppose Miss Goodbody is there, too."

"If you mean Anne Goodson, John's secretary, I really don't know if she's there or not. Why are you always implying something where she and John are concerned?"

"Because I think you are a dear, Margaret, but entirely too trusting. You know how John raves about what a wonderful secretary she is. He really says too, too much."

"Lay off, Peg. John always raves about each new employee. Everyone he hires is going to be the most perfect employee ever. He's the eternal optimist. It's part of his charm. He's like some Diogenes, looking for perfection instead of honesty."

"My, we are defensive."

"Peg, please don't sit here and drink and get *offensive*."

"Wouldn't for the world. It's much too nice a day. Barney! We're dry. Set up a couple more of these delicious things." Peggy turned back to Margaret and said, "How's your office these days?"

"You would ask. Awful, just awful."

"Is it that tiger of a boss of yours?"

"Oh, sometimes, but sometimes he is very nice." Margaret paused as Barney put down the fresh drinks. "It's really the other two women in the office. I have tried and tried to get along with them…"

"Wait a minute, sweetie." Peg put a restraining hand on Margaret's arm and turned to Barney. "Goddamn it, Barney, this is a rotten martini. You know I don't like them three to one. Dump these out and make 'em right. I spend enough good money in here to get some service."

Barney's mouth was set in a grim line, his face impassive. But he managed to get out a "Yes, ma'am."

Margaret bent her head in chagrin and ate the olive she had put aside on a napkin. She snapped the plastic toothpick in two.

Peggy seemed satisfied with Barney's swift mixing of the new drinks. She turned back to Margaret and continued, "And?"

"Well," Margaret began again, "it's really Norma and Martha. I don't think I'm a hard person to get along with. I really try. And I bite my tongue a lot and don't say what's really on my mind when they irritate me, but..." She paused and grimaced. She could hear the whine creeping into her voice. Margaret tossed her head and said more decisively, "I really don't think it's my fault. They are always complaining about me not meeting deadlines. It is true I've had some bad luck this fall. I mean, the Compton job took a long time because that idiot Larry couldn't understand English. I told him very plainly what to do, and he botched the drapes, and they had to be redone." She ate the last olive.

"Then it wasn't my fault that the order for the Hogan wallpaper got lost. It must have been the mail. I distinctly remember making out the order form and putting it in the envelope. Anyway, they both have made such a big deal about it to Mr. Evrard that he called me in the other day and was pretty severe. I didn't blame him. After all, he gets it from the customers. He was pretty nice when I explained things. But those two bitches..." Margaret's voice trailed off. She hated getting angry, even if she was in the right.

"I know, babe." Peggy was sympathetic. "Life's full of 'em. What are you going to do?"

"I can't make up my mind. One day I want to quit, and the next day I'm fine. John says whatever I want to do, he'll back me up."

"Good old John, just so long as he gets to do whatever he wants, too. Maybe you had better hang onto that job."

"What are you talking about? What's my job got to do with John?"

"Well sugar, I know you are a *practically* perfect wife, but with John-boy's penchant for the *absolutely* perfect, and if he and Miss Sweetpants are getting to be an item..."

"Goddamn it, Peggy, shut up," Margaret hissed.

"Well, I just meant, you might have to earn a living again, and—"

"Stop it!" Margaret held her glass out to Barney. "How about another round, Barn?"

The bar was crowded now. Margaret was suddenly conscious of the man at her left. He was digging the elbow of a rough Shetland jacket into her forearm, leaning away from her, deep in conversation with a companion. She felt crushed by those on her other side, too, suffocated by the smoky, stuffy air.

Barney took the glass and leaned close to Margaret, keeping his voice low. "No more, Mrs. Parkhurst. I've phoned your husband. Now don't get mad. He asked me to. The last time this happened, he said to me, 'Barney, the next time Peg comes in and gets too much to drink, you cut her off and call me.' And, ma'am, you've been sitting here alone for no more than an hour mumbling to yourself and had four martinis. That's enough for anybody, ma'am."

Margaret Parkhurst looked into the mirror. Her own face stared back from the glass. She looked sad and tired. There was only one woman reflected in the glass. The rest of the people behind the blond oak bar were men.

NORTH OF SOUTH CAROLINA

M y mother is one of those women who can write a note, couched in the proper English of a graduate from a lady-like women's college, and you can still hear the whine. So I called home.

"Seldon, darlin'."

Her inflection brought back the South Carolina Piedmont, slopes that had not quite attained the status of mountains, miles of peach orchards, and the fragrant acanthus bush that grew outside my bedroom window.

"Mama? Tell me about Aunt Kate. What have the doctors said?"

"Oh, who knows? You can't understand a thing they say, anyway. All I know is she's really not well, and you know she's never been ill a day in her life."

"How ill, Mama?"

"She's got these awful sick headaches, but the doctor says they're not migraines. She's not eating. I don't know, Seldon. I'm just worried sick myself, and of course, your brother's no help, and Mary Goddard is so busy with her family."

She paused, and in that moment of silence, some complicated process took place inside the convolutions of my own intracranial folds, and I heard myself say, "All right, Mama, I've told the office I'm taking my vacation the last two weeks in July. I'll come down for a few days."

Good God, what had I said? South Carolina in July? It would be hotter than the hinges of Hades, no ocean within a four-hour drive of where I would be, with more cousins, aunts, and uncles than I care to number, as well as my mother, my brother Hanford, and my sister Mary Goddard with all her crew. All because of that bitch, Aunt Kate, who hated me? Or at least she always gave that impression, so much so that I was continually irked at myself for an abiding interest in and even an obsession with the health and welfare of my aged relative. Unlike my charming and self-absorbed mother, Aunt Kate gave me her undivided attention and unending disapproval.

My mother did not waste a nanosecond. "Oh, darlin', I'm so relieved, I can't tell you. What day will you arrive? July what? About the fifteenth? There's a plane from New York gets in about one thirty."

How did she know all that? The fifteenth was on a Saturday, the first day of my vacation.

"I don't know, Mama." I could hear the edge of anger, the stubbornness in my reply.

"Well, call the airlines, and call me right back, darlin'." Did her tone ever change in all my life? Did she scream at me, perhaps when I was two, or was there always this implacable, granite-hard good humor?

I made another unconscious decision. "I'm going to drive, Mama. I haven't seen the countryside from here down in a long time. I'll call you from the road and let you know when I'll be in." I felt the prickle of cowardice on my neck. I knew all I was doing was playing for time. "Look," I said, "there are flashing buttons all over my phone, I've got to go."

"All right, darlin'. Now, don't drive too fast, and have a lovely trip. We're all dyin' to see you."

Aunt Kate, I thought, might be dying, but not to see me. With that, I put my family out of my mind and went back to business.

I am a bond broker. I have worked at trading for twenty-five years, and "the street" has been good to me. I can afford to pay alimony to my ex-wife, provide an expensive education for our daughter, Catherine, maintain a modest apartment in the East Fifties, and indulge my one addiction and my one secret vice. The addiction is my red Mercedes. Housing and maintenance for the small automobile in New York is obscenely expensive. The secret vice is that I am a poet. I have written much and published little. Writing keeps me sane. Not publishing drives me crazy.

Saturday, the fifteenth of July, dawned hot and hazy in New York. By 10:00 in the morning, I had packed my Mercedes 350SL and was headed south on Park Avenue toward the Lincoln Tunnel.

Instead of driving through the attenuated megalopolis bordering I-95, as soon as I entered Virginia, I went west to the spine of the Blue Ridge Mountains and only then turned south toward Spartanburg with the express intent of taking two days to make the one-long-day's drive. At Front Royal, I booked a motel room. My only prearrangement for the trip was to make lunch reservations at the Inn at Little Washington, Virginia. A first class meal makes any trip bearable.

By 4:00 the next afternoon, I was halfway from Charlotte to Spartanburg, the terrain already taking on that nostalgic familiarity of ground covered, time and again, in childhood. The home place had not changed, and the vivid beauty of crepe myrtle in full bloom was some recompense for the oppressive heat. The house, like so many in the southern coastal states, was not Federal but built in the twenties to resemble colonial homes lost to neglect, fire, or the "Wah." The Flemish bond brick was the color of good claret, and the door was surmounted by a broken pediment, painted white and topped with the traditional welcoming pineapple.

Mama was standing at the door with a glass of sweet tea in one hand and a palm fan in the other. I wondered if she had been standing there all day or just happened by as I turned into the long drive.

"Hi, darlin', I just *knew* you'd be here about this time."

How, I wondered, as I kissed her cool cheek.

"Come on in this house. Copeland will get your cases. I want to hear everything, especially about that *gorgeous* granddaughter of mine, Miss Catherine. But I'll wait 'til dinner. It's at six thirty, as usual. Aunt will want to hear it all, too, and you needn't tell it twice."

My old room was on the first floor in one of the wings. Aunt Kate's was across the hall. Her door was closed.

Mama led the way to the room, calling to Ruby Mae, the cook, to bring me a glass of tea. Copeland, Ruby Mae's husband and the handyman, brought my bags, and I began to unpack. My mother sat on the bed and, despite her promise to wait until dinner, plied me with questions about Catherine and me. Ninety percent of her inquisition was about what really was of interest her, the latest news about her granddaughter's clothes, social life, and boyfriends.

Dinner was always served promptly at six thirty, and true to old habits, I was dressed in a clean shirt and entered the dining room at that precise hour, forgetting that Aunt Kate insisted that all the clocks in the house be set five minutes ahead of Greenwich, lest the family be late for any occasion or invitation outside of the house.

The two women occupied each end of the long mahogany dining table. My place, as always, was in the middle.

Aunt Kate, whom I called simply Aunt, pronounced with a broad A, was ten years older than my mother. The sisters could not have looked less alike. Years had hardly touched my mother. At seventy, her skin was still relatively unlined and her hair was dyed almost the same color of ash blond as I first remembered. Aunt, at eighty, had absolutely white hair done in a loose bun on top of her head. As a relatively young widow of forty-five, when she came to live with us after my father died, people often remarked how much she looked like Henry Dana Gibson's drawings. There was still that slender-nosed, patrician air about her, but she looked thin and as transparent as onion skin.

"Hello, Seldon," she greeted me. "I see you are still surviving in that wretched city you choose to live in."

"And surviving very well, Aunt," I said. "I'm sure you're pleased to hear it." I gave her a perfunctory peck. She did not look directly at me. Somewhere beyond the Nina Ricci perfume, she smelled old. "Besides, you used to live in fair Gotham."

"I never liked it. Walter did."

Mother changed the subject. "Hanford was coming for dinner, but he called and said he wasn't feeling well."

"Still hung over from last night, or drunk again?" I asked before Aunt had time to make a similar remark. You're getting slow, Aunt, old girl, I thought, and gave her a smile that I hoped showed the sneer I intended. She looked at me from the corner of her eye, not giving an inch.

"Your brother is not a drunk," Mama said, in something of the same tone President Nixon used to deny he was a crook. "He said he was sick, so I choose to believe him."

"He's been drunk every Saturday and either drunk or hung over every Sunday for the last twenty years, Mama. You believe whatever you like." This was harsher than I intended.

"Now, you don't know that for a fact, and neither do I," she said.

This time I firmly changed the subject to inquire about the myriad other relatives.

Ruby Mae's cooking was as good as I remembered. Copeland served coffee after dessert, but just to Aunt and me.

"I've got to run, darlin'. Sorry to leave you, but you know I always go to your sister's on Sunday evening," Mama explained. "And I would make an exception on your first night home, but I promised the girls I would come hear all about the tennis tournament at the club. Both Amelia and Charlotte played."

"The girls" referred to my teenage nieces, one of them older and one just younger than my Catherine.

"I can just see Charlotte, the cow, in whites on the court." Aunt addressed the remark to the chandelier, but I glanced at her sharply. "The cow" was the unkind epithet Catherine always used when she spoke of her spoiled younger cousin.

My mother ignored her and excused herself from the room. "Well, I'm off to Mary Goddard's." Her voice echoed cheerily from the hall, and the front door slammed, rather hard I thought.

Aunt broke the ensuing silence.

"Don't tell me you came all the way down here to see me?"

"Yes, I actually think I did," I said.

"Why?"

"I don't really know."

For a moment she looked almost vulnerable. "I've already made the will, Seldon. And you're not in it."

"I didn't assume I was," I said.

She laughed a dry laugh. "And what's more, you don't really care, do you?"

"No, Aunt Kate, I don't care. I may not have as much money as you do, but I have all I need. Give it to the others. They seem to need it, and God knows they want it badly enough."

"Badly enough to put up with me all these thirty-five years, you mean?"

"I probably do."

"Good boy, and there's no probably to it." Her voice regained some of the martial firmness I remembered from childhood. "But now, what do you think they would have done all these years,

Seldon, without Aunt Kate to keep the pot stirred, let alone patch the roof, paint the house, keep the yard, and redecorate every few years? I think they would have dried up and blown away long ago."

"How can you dry up any faster than Hanford digging his grave with a whiskey bottle, my mother's sherry, or Mary Goddard warding off boredom with Valium?"

"Oh, there are faster ways," she said vaguely. "So, if you came to see me, how do I look?"

"Remarkably well."

"What a pity, you think. Now tell me honestly."

"Honestly? From the insinuations in Mother's note, I expected to find you on your deathbed, not at the dinner table." Copeland poured me another cup of coffee, and I stirred both cream and sugar into it.

As he left the room, she said, "But I am on my deathbed, my dear."

"From what? Spleen, as they called it in the Bard's day?"

"What did your mother tell you?" Her voice was unusually quiet.

"Something about sick headaches, a diagnosis that didn't quite square with the tone of her letter."

"God," she exploded, "that went out with fainting couches. It would have been closer to the truth to tell you I had a maggot in my brain, which you've always believed anyway."

"So what is wrong with you, Aunt?"

"One of those fancy MRI machines says I have a rather large and growing tumor in my brain." She held up her left hand that had been hidden in her lap and turned full face to me for the first time. The atrophy was apparent, as if she had had a slight stroke. The left eye drooped at the outer corner, her mouth drew downward, and most startling, the enormous diamond she always wore on her left hand was absent. Only the plain wedding band remained.

39

The surprise must have shown on my face. "I'm sorry," was all I could stammer.

She smiled a genuine smile. "Don't start being nice to me, Seldon. You'll spoil all the fun I get from your visits."

"What are you doing about it?" I asked.

"The cancer? Nothing—absolutely nothing. And to answer the nasty question everyone wants to ask, not long. I probably have only a matter of weeks, perhaps days. They never want to be too specific, but over the years I've become pretty good at outguessing Dr. Gaston, useless old fool."

"But, aren't you in pain?"

"I take back what I just said; Gaston's not a total waste. He keeps me generously supplied with anti-seizure medicine and some kind of steroid. But lately I've had headaches, so now I get the joys of morphine and Atavan. Ruby Mae gives me the shots; her daughter's an LPN at the hospital and showed her how. She's not supposed to, of course, but everybody looks the other way."

The thought of my indomitable aunt about to succumb even to death was a difficult concept for me.

"Finally, I'm a junkie," she chortled, "like everybody else in the family. Now I fit right in. And *I'm* on the really good stuff!"

"Hooray for you," I said.

Ruby Mae poked her head around the swinging door into the kitchen. Her lined brown face looked tired.

"Miz Kate, I'm goin' carry Copeland to church, now. I'll be right back an' hep you into bed. Will you be okay for your shot 'til I come back?"

"Yes, Ruby Mae, I can wait," Aunt said.

The kitchen door swung shut, and for the first time in our lives, my aunt and I sat in protracted silence, each taking an occasional sip of tepid coffee. The mantel clock in the dining room ticked a measured continuo to the random sounds of the old house and evening birdcalls. I sat staring at the cut-glass bowl of daisies my mother had placed on the mirrored plateau at the center of the table.

Finally my aunt arose. I stood as if to help.

"Stay still, Seldon." She grasped a silver-headed cane that had been on the back of her chair and set out with stiff, limping steps toward the hallway door. "At least I can still drag myself to the bathroom."

Her back was only slightly bowed between the shoulders of the black print silk blouse, its white flowers as pristine as her hair.

I finished the last of my coffee and, childlike, licked the sugar from the bottom of the Limoges cup. Then, from long habit of living alone, I took the cups to the kitchen and began to rinse them.

Through the open kitchen door, I heard her fall, a heavy thump followed by a back and forth rumble from the rockers of Grandfather's mahogany chair. The chair was in my aunt's bedroom.

I ran through the dining room and down the hall. My aunt was lying on the polished planks of the bedroom floor. In the dim evening light, I could see her lift herself on her good right arm, trying to rise. With each effort, she gave a primal grunt. Her left hand was hanging with the palm up and turned backward from her body. The left side of her face had collapsed, and spittle, red with blood, drooled onto her breasts, dying the white flowers in rusty streaks. I knelt beside her.

Her voice was a thick, angry wail. "Don't touch me! Damn! I've wet myself like a two-year-old. Let me alone. Ruby Mae'll be back shortly." Her lips fumbled over the words. She had hit her mouth against the rocker as she fell.

I pulled several tissues from her dressing table, and with her right hand, she began to blot the blood. In the bathroom I found a towel that I spread on the side of the bed. I lifted her up to sit there.

I began to unbutton her dress, and she pushed me away. "What do you think you're doing," she muttered.

"I'm going to get you out of those soiled clothes and into bed, and then I'm going to call Dr. Gaston," I said.

"You are not." Her head came up. "No man has seen me without clothes for thirty-five years," she said, "including Dr. Gaston."

"Then it's high time some man did," I said and continued to unbutton the dress.

Her good hand came up and took me firmly, even a little painfully by the chin. I looked up to see an expression in her eyes I had never seen before. It was not fear, but an intense, studying gaze.

"How could I have known?" she said.

"What?" I managed to say, my jaw still in her grip.

"You were such a little *runt*, the runtiest of the three of you when you were born."

I pulled her hand gently away. "As you can see, I did grow up, and I'm the tallest of the three of us, too."

She looked down at the reddened tissues in her lap.

"What was it you couldn't have known, Aunt?"

"That you would be the one I would always depend on."

"You never depended on anybody in your life," I said.

"You always had p. and v., as your daddy called it."

"Piss and vinegar, that's me," I said. I paused and looked down at her face. "What made you come back here when Dad died, Aunt Kate? Uncle Walter left you plenty of money. You could have stayed in New York, gone to California, traveled."

"I did travel. Mostly when you were little. Don't you remember?" She sat silently a moment, holding the tissues to her chin, staring at the rocking chair. "Where else was I to come back to?"

I pulled the dress over her head and dropped it on the floor. Despite her age and myriad wrinkles, she, like my mother, had the flawless skin of southern women who have made a fetish of staying out of the sun. I doubted if any of the present generation would be so lucky at eighty.

She waved toward the dresser and said, "Gowns are in the second drawer of the chiffonier."

I smiled at the archaic term.

When I had found a gown and put it over her head, I began to remove the rest of her clothes from under its concealing folds. Even now, I could not treat Aunt Kate in a completely cavalier way.

Her glance flicked across me and returned to the chair. Her voice continued, as soft as the yellow bands of sunlight on the floor. "And I had no children. You three were all I had to mark the future."

"Didn't Uncle Walter want children?"

"Oh yes, he actually did, but we couldn't have children, and he didn't believe in adoption. Too much of a snob, I suppose."

I found her revelation fascinating. I always thought she considered us a nuisance, but I could not find it in my heart to ask the rude questions prompted by my curiosity.

"Gonorrhea."

I thought I had misunderstood. "What?"

"Walter picked it up in Europe on his 'Grand Tour.'" She laughed softly. "It was my wedding present."

She made a wry face at the old rocking chair. "Oh, he never knew until I got sick. By then, the infection had done the damage."

I pulled off her shoes and stockings and gathered up the wet mass of clothing. I dropped it on the bathroom floor and turned down the bed. When I lifted her to move her under the covers, she was as awkwardly light as a hollow-boned bird. Her face reflected obvious pain.

The sound of Ruby Mae's soft tread preceded her into the room. "Oh dear, Miz Kate. Oh my." The needle was in her hand.

"Everything's all right, Ruby Mae," I said, "but I'm sure Miss Kate is ready for that shot."

My aunt smiled lopsidedly and held out her right arm. I gave her a good-night kiss and left the women to their evening routine.

A short telephone conversation with Dr. Gaston confirmed what I suspected. The brain cancer was advanced by the time Aunt sought help. He said he doubted if she even knew there was anything wrong until she had a seizure about six months ago. The headaches she was experiencing were a new phenomenon. He expected the end to be rapid.

I sat in the dark of the living room, the light from a half moon revealing its self-consciously accurate eighteenth-century decor. There was no sound except the Westminster chimes of the long-case clock in the hall dividing the hours into tonal quarters.

Time. How I had hated the days and hours in this house. From the day my father died when I was twelve, I could remember nothing but Hanford's bullying, Mary Goddard's complaining, and Aunt's incessant goading and prodding. Now she was about to die, and I found it curious that the children of this household were central to her occupancy. She had always treated the three of us as though she was putting us through some sort of test for which we had no instructions and no rules. Whatever we did or said, she questioned. It was defend or die, and I often felt inadequate. My final recourse was to escape South Carolina and all it represented. I made it as far north as Yale for my education and then to what I thought of as the freedom of New York.

And my mother? Where had she been all this time? Clearly she was right here, smiling her ladylike smile, ignoring what displeased her, and giving us her "suppoaht." In retrospect, it all seemed to me to be ephemeral.

"Seldon? Seldon, honey?"

"I'm here, Mama."

"For heaven's sake, what are you doing sitting here in the dark?" She circled the room, snapping on lamps, and began a detailed narrative of her visit to my sister's.

"Mama," I interrupted, "Aunt fell tonight. I talked to Dr. Gaston, and he thinks she really will die soon. Maybe within a few days, certainly within the month."

"Well, that's what I wrote you."

I didn't argue the matter. "It's funny. I feel really bad about it. I think I'm going to miss the old dragon, and what's more, she's going to miss me. She even told me about why she and Uncle Walter never had any children."

"Really?" The comment was tinder dry. "Well, now aren't you two getting cozy at this eleventh hour?" She was looking down her nose at me, and I thought I detected real irritation. "I was surprised you came down here at all."

"You wanted me to."

"Well, yes. But I didn't suspect deathbed confessions." She sat down on the camelback sofa and draped one arm along its hump. "I just wanted some support through these very trying times," she said, turning her profile to me.

I rolled my eyes at the drama in her voice.

She seemed to sense my incredulity as clearly as I was aware of the odor of her Lancome perfume. She responded with what seemed to be real heat. "You may not appreciate it, but these years have been really hard on me. I just wanted life to be nice. Your daddy always took care of everything so that nothing bad happened, and I didn't have to know about or care about anything but this house and you children. Now you know I love Sister, but she's so *domineering.* It's a terrible thing to say, but I'm looking forward to some peace and quiet. I've put up with her bossiness all this time, when all I did was open my home to her."

She paused dramatically, assuming the same profiled pose. I recrossed my feet on the ottoman with a gesture as impatient as I felt and said, "Maybe since she paid the bills, she thought she should have a say in what went on."

"She wouldn't have had to pay the bills if Mr. Gordon hadn't made those bad investments with your daddy's money," she snapped.

"Embezzlement."

"What's wrong with you, boy? Ever since you got here you've been as snappish as that old woman. That's a terrible thing to say about Mr. Gordon. He was a wonderful man from a *fine* family. Where would a town this size *be* without a banker to look after people's personal affairs?"

"Solvent," I muttered to myself.

I spent the next three days pacing the house the way I used to see the caged polar bear at the zoo measure his confining space. I went from looking in on Aunt, to the kitchen, then a meal with my mother, back to Aunt, to my room to read, to Aunt, to my mother, and so forth. My only break was a daily visit with Dr. Gaston. Mary Goddard seemed to have prematurely bequeathed the deathwatch to me. Secretly, I was glad not to have to deal with her constant chatter. Mama escaped at more and more frequent intervals to do "errands."

Oddly, my visits to Aunt became more frequent and seemed to calm her. I preferred her silence to my mother's rambling discourses. Ruby Mae's visits also gradually became more frequent as she administered Dr. Gaston's drugs.

Mama came in and out constantly, sometimes hovering over her sister, sometimes calling me out into the hall for conversation about something that seemed inane or irrelevant. Finally, I concluded her real intention was to be sure Aunt and I had little time for serious conversation.

And indeed, conversation was intermittent at best. Aunt sometimes seemed almost comatose, occasionally completely lucid, and mostly in a delicate fog induced by both the drugs and some undefined destruction taking place in her head. She was visibly weaker each day.

On Friday, she seemed particularly alert, so I pulled up a cane-bottomed chair from the dressing table and sat by the edge of the bed.

"Tell me about Catherine and what she's doing," she said.

"You haven't seen much of her since she was thirteen," I said, "but she's grown into a real beauty, at least to my taste: an all-American-looking young woman, clean and honest and straight-forward. You can see I'm not the least prejudiced."

"She writes to me." My aunt opened her good eye and gave me a direct, if slightly drugged, look. "Did you know that?"

"No, I didn't." I was genuinely surprised.

"We've kept up quite a correspondence since the summer she spent here with us. Her mother doesn't seem to mind." Aunt chuckled. "I always liked her mother. I'll never forget the first time you brought her to Spartanburg. Your mother was appalled at all that flowing hair and flowing skirt. And she always had that peculiar odor about her."

"Marijuana."

"I gathered it wasn't her perfume." There was a long pause, and I thought Aunt had fallen asleep and forgotten all about my ex-wife. "And so she finally married her psychiatrist?"

"Drug counselor. But I can't complain. He's wonderful to and with Catherine. He's even nice to me."

"How civil and ghastly." She seemed to lapse into unconsciousness.

After breakfast the next morning, she seemed much better.

"Seldon, over there on the desk—a brown folder."

I pulled out the drawer. The folder was fat with sheets of paper in no apparent order.

"My poetry. I have something else to give Catherine, but I want both of you to have the poetry."

"Poetry? I thought I was the only closet Yeats in the family. Have you published any of this?"

"Of course not."

"Do you want me to try? I mean…" I stumbled over my thoughts.

"What difference does it make?"

"I confess I've always wanted my own poetry published."

Her right eye fixed intently on me. "Didn't make any difference in the quality of what Emily Dickinson wrote," she grumbled.

She lost interest in the argument. "Read to me," she said.

I chose a poem and began to read aloud. The odor of acanthus filled the sunny room. I read one delightful poem after another, long after she had fallen asleep.

My mother entered the room with a peremptory, "Come into the hall, Seldon. I want to talk to you."

This time, my mother was genuinely and unmistakably angry.

"Seldon, what's she cooking up?"

"I don't know what you mean."

"Don't play dumb with me, Seldon. I know my sister. What are all those papers you're poring over? The next thing, she'll have you get John Welford in here, and she'll be changing her will."

"Oh, for God's sake, Mother. That's the most paranoid thing I've ever heard."

"Don't lie to me, Seldon. You never cared two pins for her, and now I can't pry you out of her room. You always were a snake, doin' just as you please all these years with never a thought for your family."

"I beg your pardon?"

"You know what I mean. Goin' up to Yale instead of W&L. Not even to Princeton. Then marrying that awful woman and having that child. Too soon, I always thought. I must say, when you were married to that wretch was the only time I was glad you didn't live in Spartanburg. But after the divorce, the least you could have done for me was move as close as Charlotte. People buy bonds in Charlotte. You could have gotten a job and been close enough to help me."

"With what, for God's sake?"

"Everything! Finances, your brother, the farm. Here I was stuck down here with no help and putting up with my beastly sister all these years. I tell you, Seldon, I won't have it. You won't steal it! I've earned every penny that old woman has, and you're not going to take it away from me now!"

So there it was. The snapping eyes, the flushed cheeks and ugly line of the mouth I had tried so hard all my life to elicit from beneath the gracious veneer. It wasn't me she cared about; it was the lifestyle. Now I knew, and I could forgive. But a residue of resentment still clung somewhere for all the years she had withheld her anger and her love.

"Believe me, Mother, the will is not in danger. Aunt Kate has given me her poetry, and that's all I want."

My mother looked at me with disbelief and sniffed, *"Poetry?"* Then she turned on her heel and stalked away down the hall.

When I reentered Aunt's room, her good eye fixed on me.

"I heard," she said, and one corner of her mouth tilted up. "I thought she'd never break down. But now that she has, I have one more trick up my sleeve."

I felt vaguely apprehensive.

"Over there in the chiffonier. Top drawer, under my step-ins."

I opened the drawer, and under the folded lingerie was a flat gray velvet box.

"Bring it here. Open it."

Inside the box lay an exquisite Tiffany necklace and bracelet of diamonds and platinum. The huge diamond ring was there, also.

"I gave the pearls to Mary Goddard years ago. Got tired of her pestering me for them. But these are for Catherine, and it's *in the will.* You get the pleasure of paying the gift tax on them, and you get Grandfather's rocker."

"Thanks a lot," I said.

"You'll have the time of your life, and it'll be worth every penny, because when they find the jewelry is gone, the fireworks should be spectacular. Now put the baubles in your pocket and the box where you found it. Your mother checks every once in a while when she thinks I'm asleep."

I replaced the box and sat down again by the bed. The two of us laughed suppressed laughter, like naughty children, until the tears came.

Ruby Mae looked at us suspiciously when she brought the next injection. Then she smiled to herself, patted Aunt's hand, and bent and gave her a kiss. "All done?"

"All done, Ruby Mae," Aunt Kate said, and both women chuckled.

Evening stretched into night, and night thinned toward dawn. Aunt had not stirred, and her breathing grew more and more shallow. I fell asleep in the rocking chair listening to the slowing rhythm.

When I awoke at six thirty, she was dead, the jaw slack, eyes half open and rolled back. I closed her eyelids and pulled the quilt over her face. The white hair was still soft and springy.

I picked up the folder of poems and paused at the door. I said, "I love you."

The hall was dim, colors still indistinct. There were smells of bacon, coffee, and biscuits and distant sounds of Ruby Mae in the kitchen. Copeland had come over from their house, and I could hear his voice, then hers.

I put the poems in the bottom of my suitcase and felt the cold metal of the jewelry in my pocket. I ran the edge of my thumbnail over the incredible smoothness of the diamond's table, as hard and enduring and brilliant as the woman who had worn and loved it. I began to put my few belongings in the suitcase, knowing my next visit would only be after my mother's death.

Copeland and Ruby Mae would help me call the funeral home and the minister. She could select appropriate burial clothes. I would also call John Welford, but I would not wait for the services or the reading of the will. Aunt considered funerals barbaric, and we had performed our own final rituals in private.

Instead, I thought I would spend the rest of my vacation somewhere along the way to New York, at a mountain inn in the Shenandoah. I had never tried to write anything other than poetry, but I had made up my mind. Aunt deserved her own story.

HOUSES OF BONDAGE

J ewel Mae looked out of the front bedroom window, past the broad shoulder of the young man sitting on the porch. The sparse grass, burned dun brown by the August heat, barely moved. Eighth Street, east of Lottie Avenue, wasn't paved, and dust lifted slightly from the street's surface, stirred by the last cool breeze before the morning sun turned the air into a furnace.

If it wasn't Nigger Town, she thought, the street would be paved. She buttoned the last oyster shell button on her starched white uniform.

"You got enough lemonade out there, baby?" she called through the door.

"Yes, Mama."

She ticked off a mental list: he had his noon sandwich within reach, covered by a napkin to keep the flies off; he had the radio, one pitcher of water, one of lemonade, and his urinal within reach. She had made the sandwich as she fed him breakfast and cleaned the urinal after helping him dress and hoisting his body into the rusty wheelchair. She was used to the sight of his dead legs, but her heart twisted every morning at this ritual.

The sandwich was almost the last of the peanut butter, but this was Tuesday and Mrs. Carter would pay her Friday at the end of the day. Part of the five-dollar bill would be spent at Leo's grocery to replenish the larder. It was the middle of the month, so this week she didn't have either rent or life insurance to pay. There was no phone, and she had paid the electric bill last week.

The screened door banged behind her. "Now if it gets too hot, you roll yourself into the house, hear?"

"I'm okay, Mama."

He didn't change expression as she stooped to kiss him good-bye.

The ten-block walk to the Carters' house was bearable this morning. It would be hot enough to take her breath away when she walked back after 5:00 in the afternoon. This morning, the old men were already at Stiles Circle Park playing checkers, red coke bottle caps against blue cream soda tops.

"How you doin', Miz Jewel?" Mr. Johnson called out to her from the checker game, and she gave him a smile and a friendly wave. Later in the day, there would be too many younger men around the game board. The old men would have sought a nap or at least more shade. The younger men would have returned from another day of piecework or looking for any work at all. It was hard times. The White Folks called it "the Depression," but all Jewel Mae knew was that life certainly was depressing. She couldn't let herself dwell on the lack of money and her son James. He had been the apple of her eye, and she had hoped that as the star football player at Dunbar High School, he might be good enough to get into college somewhere, maybe even Hampton Institute. The broken spine put an end to that dream.

Crossing Thirteenth Street was like stepping into Fairyland. The houses on the north side of the street were four stories with basements and attics, unlike her modest bungalow. The streetcar ran down the middle of the street, its steel rails slicing like a knife the separate worlds of Jewel Mae and her employer, Mrs. Carter. The walk to work seemed to Jewel Mae like cutting a layer cake: south of Tenth only black folks, north of Tenth all white, south of Thirteenth everybody poor, north of Thirteenth rich folks.

She shifted her worn yellow leather handbag to the other hand. A purple umbrella was wedged between the handles. No rain was forecast, but the shade would help a little against the sun on the walk home. The umbrella reminded her of the one carried by Little Black Sambo in Kitty Carter's storybook. At least in summer she didn't have to combat the freezing wind, and the brown galoshes Mrs. Carter had given her were so worn they didn't keep her feet all that dry.

Jewel Mae walked up to the back door and rapped on the glass. The figure of a tall woman materialized behind a dotted Swiss curtain. The curtain moved, a green eye and a few dark curls appeared briefly, and then the door opened.

"Good morning, Jewel Mae. Come in this house."

"'Mornin', Miz Carter."

"How's James today?"

"He's doin' good."

The lady of the house asked the same question each morning and Jewel Mae said "fine" or gave an answer something like she had today. She put her purse and umbrella in the closet in the refrigerator room behind the kitchen. Mrs. Carter had already disappeared upstairs. Today was the day she went to Junior League meeting. The breakfast dishes were in the sink: Mrs. Carter's small plate held crumbs of toast, Kitty's bowl the last of the milk from her cereal. Robert must still be asleep. Mr. Carter's plate at the bottom of the pile still had traces of fried egg and grease from bacon clinging to it. Jewel Mae knew Mrs. Carter hated cooking the same thing each morning. Sometimes Mrs. C grumbled about it or complained that grease had spattered and burned her arm.

Jewel Mae took an enamel dishpan from under the sink, ran the water, tipped up the bottle of Palmolive soap, and washed the dishes. She put them in a wire drainer to dry and went to the back hall for the basket of clean laundry. Today, she would iron and take the sheets to the basement to press them on the Maytag mangle. She hated the ironing but rather liked pressing the flat sheets and pillowcases. The basement was several degrees cooler than the rest of the house, even though the mangle was hot.

Mondays, she washed clothes in the basement, hung them outside to dry, and on hot days like this took them down midafternoon before the dust could settle too heavily on them. Today, Tuesday, she ironed. Tomorrow, she would clean the downstairs and the basement. Thursdays, she cleaned upstairs, and on Fridays she did whatever chores Mrs. Carter set for her: windows, polishing silver, rearranging closets. Today, she would have to look after Kitty, too, since her mother would be gone most of the day. She never minded this part of her job. She loved the five-year-old and had taken care of her since she was a baby. Kitty would be six in August and in school all day come September. Jewel Mae would miss the child.

Robert, dressed in a cotton shirt, khaki shorts, knee socks, and oxfords, came into the breakfast room.

"Hi, Jewel Mae. Can I have some toast and cereal?"

"Mornin', Mr. Robert. You want Wheaties or Corn Flakes?"

"Gotta have a breakfast of champions," he said.

She set a place at the table with a placemat, bowl and spoon, and a cotton napkin. She brought the Wheaties box and a bottle of milk to the table. He poured cereal and began to read the cereal box, absorbing the information printed there about some athlete.

When he was through, he left the table, tossing a belated "thanks" over his shoulder. She knew he would go upstairs, brush his teeth, come downstairs, and she would hear the glass door slam. He would be gone off all day on his bicycle. She wondered what he did all day. On cooler days in the spring and fall, she could see the boys in the neighborhood playing baseball in the vacant lot next door. The one thing she knew was that he was sneaking cigarettes. His clothes smelled. She shrugged. It wasn't her problem.

Jewel Mae pulled the dishpan from under the sink and repeated the dishwashing rite. When she was through, she filled the old vinegar bottle with warm tap water, putting the aluminum plug with the holes in it into the neck of the bottle. She methodically dampened the sheets and cotton clothes, rolling each item into a small bundle to distribute the water evenly in the cloth and keep it damp during the hours of ironing. She dampened Mr. Carter's linen handkerchiefs and the cotton table napkins and stacked them in a bundle before rolling them. She would save them for last. They were easy, and she loved seeing them smooth out into perfectly flat squares. The rest of the ironing she hated. She was grateful Mr. Carter took his white cotton shirts to the laundry.

Looking cool in a black silk dress with white polka dots, its short, puffed sleeves and neck edged with stiff white linen collar and cuffs, Mrs. Carter came into the kitchen. She put her black patent leather purse and white cotton gloves on the counter and turned to Jewel Mae. Her face was apologetic and earnest under the dark curls and small straw hat.

"I'm off to the meeting, Jewel Mae. There's a hen in the Frigidaire; would you please put it on to roast about four thirty? I won't be back until five today, and you know Mr. Carter likes his dinner right at six. You might put an apple in the cavity. I don't think we want any stuffing in it."

"Yes, ma'am. Be glad to."

"Thanks. I hope Robert gets home on time today," she said, as much to herself as to Jewel Mae.

The glass door closed, and the sound of Mrs. Carter's white high-heeled shoes tapped decisively across the breezeway to the garage. The 1934 Packard made a smooth, purring sound.

So the lady of the house was off for her day out. While she put the now dry dishes away and cleaned the stove, Jewel Mae indulged herself in thinking about her employers. Mr. Carter was kind enough to her, but reticent and precise. He was a banker, and Jewel Mae remembered the early days of the Depression when there was enough tension in the house that she though the brick walls would explode. The Carters talked in hushed tones to each other when the children weren't around. Those were the days before Calvin passed and before Jimmy's accident, and she stayed until seven in the evening and cooked dinner for the Carters. Voices were easily overheard in the kitchen from the master bedroom just above it. Sometimes before supper, when she was still staying late or if the Carters had not yet had breakfast, she could hear Mrs. C's voice shrill, the words indistinguishable. Mr. C's voice would rumble in answer. In front of Jewel Mae or the children, they were invariably polite to each other. But there were the bruises. Jewel Mae saw them more than once on Mrs. Carter's arms and once on her cheekbone and chin.

"None of my business," she said sternly to herself.

Jewel Mae knew there was talk of the City Bank failing. She sometimes read the newspaper Mr. Carter left on the breakfast table. If the bank failed, perhaps Mrs. Carter could go back to teaching school. After all, married women were now hired by the School Board. Mrs. Carter had stopped teaching when she married, even though it was six years before Robert came along. Jewel Mae heard enough to know Mr. Carter was vehemently opposed to his wife doing that, even if it meant they would have to live on savings. Jewel Mae prayed it wouldn't happen, because household help would probably be the first place to economize. Nevertheless, she thought Mrs. Carter was secretly disappointed. She seemed to rattle around in the big house, cleaning things that didn't need cleaning, reading, going to her book club, and chairing the PTA and, of course, the Junior League. There was something about her behavior that reminded Jewel Mae of the frustrated young men who hung around Stiles Park in the afternoon.

Almost the same age as her employer, Jewel Mae thought about all the things her mother had to do that even Mrs. Carter's mother would have done. Cloth was no longer spun and woven, but all the clothes were made at home. There was water to draw, wood to cut for the stove, and the garden to tend for the kitchen. Jewel Mae had more to do each day than she could get done, but even she didn't have to do anything but light the kerosene in the stove at home and the gas Magic Chef here. There were days she envied Mrs. Carter's freedom from chores and days she thought the woman was as trapped in her life as she was.

She shook her head as she pulled the ironing board down from its cupboard in the kitchen and plugged in the heavy iron.

A small whirlwind of dimples and curls flew into the kitchen and clutched her thigh.

"Hi, Jewel Mae."

"Watch the hot iron, baby. How you doin' this day?"

"Come play Old Maid with me. Please. Please."

"Can't, sweet Kitty. Gotta iron, but we'll play one game right after lunch. Okay?"

"Okay. I'll read. Mamma got me a new Raggedy Ann book."

Kitty had always been a pliable child, maybe because she was a girl, but Jewel Mae doubted it. And while she ironed, she allowed herself to think about Ruthie. The winter she left had been a hard one. After twenty years of living together, most of it good, some of it stormy, Calvin, Ruthie and Jimmy's father, had been killed in an accident at the packing plant. The folks at the Wilson plant had been kind enough, and she was given a little money. That and the small life insurance policy Calvin had would have been all right, but that was also the fall of Jimmy's accident. Ruthie, a senior in high school, chose that January to run off with her boyfriend. She had never been a docile child, and now the prospect of being tied to her mother and her brother and helping to make a living was more than her independent spirit could bear.

Jewel Mae knew how the girl felt, but it clutched at her heart to think of her daughter, now with a daughter of her own, abandoned in Kansas City. Ruthie still preferred to shift for herself rather than come home and face the double problem of a paralyzed brother and a year-old baby. Still, Jewel Mae longed to see that baby and take care of her, at least when she had time. Maybe Ruthie was right. Maybe when the baby was older. Maybe God had other plans. She said a prayer and began to sing "Swing Low Sweet Chariot" to herself.

Singing was her solace. She worked her way though a repertoire of spirituals as she worked through the basket of ironing. She would leave the sheets and pillowcases to press on the mangle until afternoon in the cool basement. The air in the kitchen was already becoming almost more than she could take, the heat intensified by the hot iron.

Although she had not finished the napkins and handkerchiefs, she set the iron on the back of the stove to cool and began to make Kitty a peanut butter and grape jelly sandwich. She made another for herself and put some potato chips on the plates.

Kitty had a tall glass of milk and Jewel Mae a bottle of Coca-Cola from the refrigerator. After lunch, they played one game of Old Maid, and since Kitty lost, she wheedled another game out of Jewel Mae, who let her win, not trying to rid her hand of the black card.

"Let's read," Kitty said.

"One short book. I got more ironing to do and got to go to the basement and do the sheets."

They went up to the little girl's room, cool and dark on the north side of the house. Purple violets and bright green leaves on white chintz reflected what light there was with the shades drawn against the summer heat. The expandable shutters in the sash window admitted a lame breeze. Jewel Mae turned on the lamp and sat in the white painted rocking chair. Kitty climbed onto her lap, and Jewel Mae felt the girl's head snuggle against her breasts. Kitty's hair smelled of sun and her skin of Camay soap. She felt a surge of love for this child. She placed the softest of kisses on the blond curls and thought about the granddaughter in Kansas City.

"Now We Are Six," she read the title and began to read the poems in the book out loud. Kitty, who could already read and wouldn't be six until next month, read along with her, sometimes stopping to make a comment about the line drawings that accompanied the text.

Jewel Mae was about to call a halt to the reading and suggest a nap for the girl when she heard the glass door in the breakfast room slam. Robert ran up the stairs to the second floor. She could hear him gasping for breath. He went into the bathroom at the end on the hall and shut the door hard. The lock clicked.

"Get down, honey. I gotta see about your brother."

Kitty slid off her lap and headed toward the closed bathroom door, evidently as curious as Jewel Mae.

"Robert? You okay?"

No answer.

"Robert? You sick, boy?"

"No. Go away."

Jewel Mae thought he might be having bowel trouble and needed his privacy, so she turned Kitty toward her bedroom.

"Jewel Mae?" The boy's voice was muted, pleading.

"Yes, Robert."

"I guess I need some help." The lock clicked and the door opened slowly. The boy was a mess. His cotton shirt was torn at the shoulder and his khaki shorts at the knee. He was bleeding from the nose and lips, and his left eye would be blackened for some time.

"Bobby," Kitty breathed in horror.

"What happened, Mr. Robert?" Jewel Mae's voice was stern.

"I fell off my bike going over the railroad tracks." His voice was steady as he made the statement, but he didn't meet her eyes.

"Kitty, you get yourself off for a nap. Your brother's fine. I'll get him fixed up here."

The little girl trailed off reluctantly to her room, looking over her shoulder.

"And close the door, and get into bed."

Jewel Mae turned her attention to the boy. There was a gash above the black eye. She took cotton and some alcohol from the cabinet next to the pedestal sink. "This is going to sting." He winced as she cleaned the wound and put a Band-Aid on it, pushing the edges of skin together. "That's going to be some shiner, and you might even need a stitch. We'll see." She took a washcloth from the linen cupboard and rinsed it in cold water. "Here, hold this to your nose and mouth. Do you need some cotton for that nosebleed?"

He shook his head, dabbing his face with the cloth. She could see another bruise appearing on his jawline.

None of my business, she thought, but heard herself saying, "Looks to me like you been in a fight, boy."

He didn't look up but blushed slightly.

"So what do you think? The bicycle story might satisfy your mama, but I don't think your daddy will be fooled a bit."

Robert looked up. All the preteen bravado gone, real fear was in his eyes. "He'll take the belt to me good."

She sat down on the closed lid of the commode so that she could look up into the boy's face. She took him by the shoulders. "You hear me, boy. Don't you tell a story to your father. He'll take after you all the more for lying. You hear?"

He just looked at her.

"You listenin', boy?"

Finally he nodded. "I hear you."

"Now get on into your room. You need some quiet rest, too. I gotta finish the ironin' and your mama'll be home directly."

She headed back to the kitchen, plugged in the iron and finished the linens she had left until last, but the satisfaction of the smooth cloth could not assuage her troubled thoughts.

What was it with men? The only way they knew how to settle most things was a fight—fists, knives, guns, or whatever. And now in Mr. C's newspaper, there were all those stories about the possibility of war somewhere she couldn't remember.

She shook her head. She had been so glad when Jimmy decided to take all that aggression out in football, and look what that had gotten him. She brushed back a tear, put away the iron and went to the basement. Halfway through the chore, she remembered to put the chicken on to roast.

From the cool of the cement-lined room, she heard Mrs. C come in, and she knew Robert was talking to her. Jewel Mae wondered if he had decided to be honest with his mother. She hoped he had. When she finished the sheets and pillowcases, it was nearly 5:00. She unplugged the Maytag mangle and pushed it to the side of the room. She carried the ironed clothes upstairs. She put the linens in the hall closet and took the other clothes to each of the bedrooms. Kitty was playing dolls on the floor of her room, and Robert was lying on his bed listening to the little Bakelite radio he kept on the night table. He didn't look up as she put the items in his dresser. Mrs. Carter was sitting at her polished dressing table staring in the mirror, her chin in her hand. Jewel Mae had the feeling she was not looking at herself or anything in particular.

"Thank you, Jewel Mae," she said as the drawers opened and closed, never looking up.

"Miz Carter? I'm all through and goin' home."

"Fine, Jewel Mae. I'll see you tomorrow." The tone was distracted. Then the woman turned and fixed weary green eyes on Jewel

Mae. "Great way to end the day," Mrs. Carter said, her voice soft and conspiratorial.

Jewel Mae nodded in sympathy.

She retrieved her purse and umbrella from the downstairs closet and walked home the way she had come. The purple umbrella provided some shade, but the air was hot enough to pull the breath out of her. There weren't many young men or anyone else around Stiles Circle.

Jimmy wasn't on the porch. He had rolled his wheelchair inside, out of the heat. The sandwich plate and glass were empty, the pitcher almost so. The napkin had blown under the table. He had taken the urinal inside with him. She picked up the napkin, pitcher, glass and plate, clutching them in her left hand, the yellow purse dangling from her arm. With her right hand, she clutched the umbrella handle with her index finger free enough to open the screen door. The front room was marginally cooler. Jimmy was silhouetted against the open door of his bedroom.

"Hey, baby. How did you get along today?"

"Same as always, Mama. But I do need the bathroom."

"I'll be right with you, honey."

She went to the kitchen, put the dishes in the sink, and, stifling a sigh, wondered briefly if there was enough leftover macaroni and cheese for supper.

CROSSWORD

In daylight, the opulent midtown apartment had the impersonal cool appearance of an *Architectural Digest* layout—white, gray, and black, with chrome and marble accents. Despite the occasional book or vase of flowers, it did not seem to be lived in. Even the bedroom rarely looked rumpled. At night, the aspect changed, but more in atmosphere than appearance.

If the couple had bothered to look out of the huge windows that formed the corner of the room in which they were sitting, they would have been afforded a spectacular view of Manhattan at night with millions of lights, tiny as Christmas bulbs, outlining the pattern of towers. As it was, they sat in matching black leather chairs of Scandinavian design, each with its own ottoman. The three sources of light in the room, other than the blinking lights of the city, were matching chrome-shaded halogen bulbs that spread, like branches of a tree, from a round marble base, and a television set.

An insect was eating another insect on the television screen. The voice of the narrator was soothing as he explained what could be described as either the vagaries of nature or its rawest aspect.

The man, tieless and with his stocking feet crossed on the ottoman, was dressed in dark suit trousers and a white shirt, open at the collar. A volume of the latest biography of Harry Truman lay open on his lap, and he divided his attention between the pages and the television screen.

The woman, in a pale skirt and sweater, sat with her feet tucked under her. She was unfashionably plump, the only object in the room that seemed to be, by some elusive measurement, out of place. *The New York Times* was folded so that she could work the crossword puzzle. After having filled in a third of the squares, she determined that the subject of today's puzzle was the seven deadly sins. "Pride" and "greed" had already appeared with the strokes of her ballpoint pen. Now she filled in the long vertical line with the three words of the subject.

"What time does your plane leave in the morning?" she asked as she inked in the final letters.

"Early," he answered, glancing from his book to the television. "The car is picking me up at five thirty."

"Move around quietly," she said with a touch of acid. She added in a more matter-of-fact tone, "Is Carla Mandeville going with you?"

"I'm not sure," he said, eyes once again on the page of his book. "The last time I talked to her, she thought the project with Kodak would keep her here."

"That must be disappointing."

"Everyone at the office wants to go to this meeting," he said.

The colorful picture on the television showed a frog eating something that flew too close to its long tongue.

The woman filled in "gluttony" and reached for a foil-wrapped chocolate kiss from the small Steuben bowl at her elbow. She unwrapped the confection, put it in her mouth, rolled the foil into a ball the size of BB shot, and dropped it back into the bowl, all without lifting her eyes from the newspaper. The man also moved automatically and took a swallow of Armagnac from the snifter on his side of the table. Just as he set the glass down, the cordless telephone next to it rang.

"Hello?" The tone was crisp, the sound of an executive, then changed. "Oh, hi."

At the change in his voice, the woman glanced up with interest and anticipation. Their daughter and only child lived in San Francisco and often called at about this hour.

The man put the book on the ottoman, carefully marking the place with a metal bookmark.

"I don't know. Let me go into the study and check my briefcase."

He crossed the room and switched on the light in a small room off the living room. He closed the door behind him.

The woman's face slowly jelled into an indifferent mask as she realized the caller was not their daughter. She continued with the puzzle but could hear his voice. He laughed. The words were indistinguishable. The cadence had a lilt.

She watched intently as a larger fish relentlessly pursued a smaller one across the screen. The large fish prevailed.

"Got 'im. Persistence pays off!" she addressed the silent television. Then she frowned and said to the space between the chair and the screen. "I should have finished school. I could have done an MBA. I'm smart enough."

She went back to the puzzle and filled in "sloth."

"Envy" appeared in the squares about the time the man returned to his chair, put down the silent phone and took up the book without comment.

"Carla?"

"Yes."

"Good news, I gather."

"Very. Kodak agreed to the proposal." There was a note of triumph in his voice. "She's certainly done an excellent job on that one."

"Anger" appeared in the puzzle.

"I suppose she's going to the meeting then."

"Yes."

The woman's fingers shifted the pen until she grasped it in her fist like a knife, her arm drawn back as if to strike a blow, but she did not turn to face him. She clenched her jaw, and the faintest scream died in her throat. Instead, she feigned a cough and turned the pen once more toward the newspaper, the instrument gripped so tightly that the blood in her forefinger disappeared from the nail bed beneath her clear nail polish. With deliberation, she filled in sixty-three and sixty-five down.

The crossword in the bottom line was "lust."

CRYPTOQUOTE

Carla Mandeville felt happier than she had in years, walking down the street in front of Rockefeller Center the week before Christmas. The sky was a crisp blue, the breeze just chilly enough, and New Yorkers were smiling.

Carla smiled back in response. "How could you not be happy?" she asked herself.

It had been a rough eight months, most of which she had definitely spent in a fit of depression.

"Self-inflicted," she thought, and her smile took on an edge of irony.

First, she had changed jobs, going from a rising career with a nationally known manufacturing firm to a small office that handled the legal work for a midwestern maker of plastic buttons. Privately, she referred to her bosses as "two eye and four eye," since one wore glasses and one did not, and they were both obsessed with the button business. Actually, she enjoyed the association with the rather staid members of the staff and sometimes thought her hard-earned MBA was put to better use here than in the more high-profile job.

The real reason for her change of venue and her depression was her former boss. They had challenged that most sacred of office rules against employee fraternization and been lovers. Her father inelegantly dubbed it, "Dipping your pen into the company inkwell." At least with him, she had hoped for some sympathy.

Neither of her parents showed the slightest compassion for her predicament. Her mother remarked that such was the wages of sin, making it clear that she disapproved less of the moral part of the dilemma than the fact that sin seemed to create such a mess. It was just impractical!

As a result, Carla poured all her tears and woes onto the shoulder and into the ear of her best friend, Janey. In fact, she was on her way to meet Janey now at a soup-and-sandwich place they liked. At the thought of her friend, she smiled again in pure delight. The smile was short lived.

Just ahead of her walked a couple with two children. The age of the couple marked them as grandparents rather than parents. The man was handsome, still lithe, but well past fifty. He wore a dark suit covered by a navy-blue cashmere topcoat. A soft fedora framed his bony face with its black and silver sideburns. The woman, approximately the same age, could be charitably described as matronly.

Carla was surprised to find herself inclined to charity as she watched the woman, who was swathed in a full-length mink coat that added to her bulk. She was having an animated conversation with a girl of about ten. Both of them were laughing at some private remark, and the man, holding the hand of a boy, younger than the girl, was obviously enjoying the conversation.

Carla's stomach lurched. She had not seen the man since she left the firm, but there he was, with the wife he professed to dislike. The wife who he insisted had nothing in common with him. The wife Carla had pled with him to divorce. The wife he refused to leave.

So the grandchildren were in town for Christmas. "Good God," Carla thought, "they look like something out of a Norman Rockwell." But there was more to it than that. The woman's pleasure was so genuine it was almost palpable. What was more, the man seemed fully engaged with her and with the children.

Carla slowed her steps, letting the holiday crowd fill a gap between herself and the four people. Finally, all she could see was unfamiliar bobbing heads in winter caps.

She turned the corner toward her destination and stopped at a newsstand to buy a copy of her hometown newspaper. She was ordinarily disinterested in the reports of people and events that seemed to her far removed from the reality of New York City, but it gave her a sense of being closer to her parents. Also, she was addicted to the cryptoquote printed in the paper each day. There was something about deciphering the code that took her back to teenage fantasies of being a CIA agent.

When she reached the restaurant, she took a table and waited for her friend. She scanned the news in the paper, checked the obituaries, and folded the pages so that she could work the puzzle.

She had barely begun when Janey came into the restaurant. The two women could not have looked more dissimilar. Carla was small, rather delicate, and always dressed in a business suit. Janey was tall but not raw boned. Instead, her figure was filled out by the rather blowzy, one-of-a-kind wearable art outfits that looked entirely at home in SoHo, where she worked. She also lived there in a minuscule one-room apartment with the shower in the middle of the living space.

"So how goes it?" Janey said.

"Fine." Carla put down the pen and the puzzle, but barely glanced up.

"Really? You don't look to me like you have much of the Christmas spirit. I think NYC is full of it this time of year—kids, shoppers, skaters, you know."

If Carla had considered delaying her encounter, or omitting it altogether from her conversation with Janey, that changed instantly.

"I saw you-know-who, his wife, and his two grandchildren on the way over here," she said, using Janey's epithet for the man. Janey had always referred to him as a man with no name. She insisted his behavior did not rise to the dignity of a name or title. Originally, Carla had gone along because she did not want some casual reference to be overheard when the friends lunched or met for a drink. Today she used it because she was feeling a peculiar sensc of distance from him.

"They looked like something off a Christmas card."

Janey let the silence lie undisturbed for a beat or two. "How did that make you feel?'

Sometimes Carla thought Janey took her speech directly from *Peanuts*. Complete with a "Lucy, the doctor, is in" tone of voice.

She answered with a mixture of irritation, bewilderment, and curiosity. "I felt sympathy for her, anger at him, and generally not much of anything for me, even pain."

"Good show!" This time with a broad British accent. "I think you're getting over it, love."

Carla shrugged and rose from the table. The women left her paper and their coats to mark the table, took their purses, and went to the buffet line.

Halfway through lunch, all the other mutual gossip having been disposed of, the subject returned to Carla's encounter.

"You know," she mused, "I got to thinking about all my mother's fussing about that affair. She knew from the beginning it wouldn't work out, but instead of giving me a hard time about sinning with a married man, she harped on the messiness of it all: the hiding and sneaking, the lonely holidays, all that. I thought secretly what she was really bitching about was the prospect of no grandchildren. She may have had a point."

"How so?"

"Just looking at that woman today with those kids, it was pretty special. I couldn't summon up any of those old feelings of frustration or envy. All I could think of was that she deserved every second of what was happening."

"Earned it, more like. For living with the bastard all these years."

"Maybe." She paused. "And you know what? He was genuinely into it, too."

"Could have told you that. They always complain about the wife, but when it comes to knowing what makes them comfortable at home, all that image stuff they love, the great apartment, the right car, wifey has the edge. All they really want is a little on the side."

"Oh, for God's sake, Janey, let's not go back to the old 'all they do is think with their prick' argument. We did have something real besides the sex."

"Well, you had a lot of common interests. I grant you that. But for him, I would lay down my last ducat, the sex was about 99 percent of the attraction."

"I did love him," she said, using the past tense unconsciously, "and he said he loved me."

"Both probably true. And that and a buck-fifty gets you a cup of coffee in this place." Janey had to get back to the shop where she worked and began to gather up her purse and coat.

Carla had one more observation she wanted to make. "You know what gets to affairs like ours? Not the lying and hiding, not the obligations still owed to the other family, and not the lack of commitment, whatever that is. It's the history. That's our lives. That's the kind of stuff my parents have I could never understand growing up. They're so different, and they fight all the time. But the history is real." She felt as though she had been pontificating.

Janey halted in her preparations to leave and looked Carla straight in the face. "Righto. And that's what your old buddy's wife knew all the time. You're kidding yourself if you think she didn't know all about your little twosome. But, as you say, she had the history. All she had to do was hang on until you either saw the light or he got bored—which he has probably done before, anyway."

"But," Janey continued, "that's neither here nor there. What do you want, Carla? Those kids and Christmastime? A relationship that may not be the greatest and certainly isn't the grand passion you imagined with him? Is that what you want?"

"I guess it is."

"Then you have to do something about it. I've been trying to get you to go out with my friend, Frank. Do it! Stop sitting home by yourself."

"Oh, don't start with Frank."

"Yes, do start with Frank. You have to start someplace."

"Okay, okay, you win. Tell him to call."

Janey gave her a hug and kiss, accompanied by a triumphant smile.

Carla decided to delay her return to the office. Something about what Janey said rankled. What did she want? Did she know? She thought the great job, the MBA, and the love of her life were what she wanted. She had none of that now, except the degree, and she knew she was more satisfied than she had been in her former job. Maybe it was time she did some serious thinking about herself and her goals, unencumbered with the expectations of family, society, or even her own preconceived ideas. The thought of looking that deep inside frightened her.

She got a refill on her coffee and began the puzzle. "Pns mcds kncqn cf gxsltzcxsv cf xrp krjwpn mchcxb—ymtpr." This was an unusually short aphorism, and it didn't have many repeated letters. The *e*'s were usually the best place to start. She guessed that the first word was "The" and soon worked out the author's name.

The coffee was still warm in the cup when she was finished. She stared at the paper. That certainly described her old boss. She didn't want it to describe Carla Mandeville.

"The life which is unexamined is not worth living—Plato."

THE WHITE KID GLOVES

Elena Yvgenskaya Miller stared out of the window of the E train, wishing the ride from her Queens apartment to midtown Manhattan was longer. A ghostly image of her face, like a dim hologram, stared back at her from the sooty window of the subway. She wasn't sure she was ready for the encounter. Surely, it would be innocuous enough. In fact, her mind was three-quarters made up to reject the offer, despite the lure of the money.

She smiled at the thought. Did this make her more or less of an American? She believed the almost thirty years she had now spent in the United States had thoroughly acculturated her. She dressed smartly; her English had steadily improved and had become thoroughly idiomatic over the years, thanks to early training from a half-British mother and two decades as a simultaneous translator for the United Nations. There were also the twenty-five years with her very literate husband, Clarke Miller. Sometimes, she thought his Harvard degree and erudition were the chief reasons she had married him. If the marriage had not been passionate, it was, at the very least, satisfying.

She knew she had been incredibly lucky. Actually, she married the first person who asked her at a time when she felt she was drowning in the complexities of a new country with no means of support. The marriage ended suddenly about five years ago when Clarke died within six months after colon cancer was diagnosed.

She missed him. Most importantly to Elena, he had been a loving and interested father to Greg and to Tanya.

Elena always felt a rush of warmth when she thought of her children. Tall Greg, married now to Karen with two thoroughly American children, Katy and John. She privately referred to them as Gregor, Katya, and Sascha.

Tanya, Harvard graduate like her father, seemed more Russian, or at least more familiar to Elena than Greg. Tanya was in South Africa at the moment, working as an assistant to the Episcopal Bishop in a rural diocese. There was something of her adventurous great-grandmother, who followed her heart from London to St. Petersburg, and of Elena's own risk-taking nature, which brought her to the United States.

Earlier, standing on the platform that afternoon, Elena was reminded of that blustery day in Berlin, the day she left the tight, and to her stultifying, circle of Russian life. Elena was a defector.

She looked down at her feet, set primly side by side barely under the seat in front of her. She had slender but muscular legs and long feet. Those feet, now wearing a pair of black Gucci pumps, at one time wore satin shoes that felt like a second skin, the ankles meticulously wrapped in ribbons. At one time, Elena danced at the Kirov Ballet.

That was how she happened to be in East Berlin and how she happened to be a defector—a simple story. The complications began at the moment of her crossing from one life to the next. It was a strange kind of rebirth.

Her concentration jumped from the familiarity of the past to the unpredictability of the future. What sort of offer would this man make? Why was she even tempted?

His English, only moderately inflected with the flavors of samovars, vodka, and borscht, was precise and evocative when she answered the phone.

"Mrs. Miller?"

"Yes?"

"My name is Mischa Ulanov."

The very ordinariness of the name made the letters KGB flash through her mind. Paranoia ingrained from childhood dies hard.

He continued, informing her that a mutual friend had given her name to him, someone she barely remembered from her earliest days in the United States. She did not respond.

"Mrs. Miller, I understand you have recently left your position at the UN, no?"

"Yes." Elena felt a deep reluctance to reveal more than monosyllables would convey.

"Mrs. Miller, I have a proposition of business to make to you." She smiled at the syntax. "I am a businessman from Leningrad— St. Petersburg—and I need someone to establish and maintain a small office for me in New York City. Not a difficult job and not one that would be full employment. For now, a clearinghouse, really. Then, if my business prospers here, I will enlarge the office here in the United States."

He paused, but she did not respond.

"My *problema* is to find someone for about six months to be transition. I would pay well and hope you are interested."

The amount of salary he mentioned made her gasp. "What sort of business are you in?"

She asked the question in Russian. He answered in the same language, explaining—in what she thought were rather vague terms—an import-export business. Drugs? Contraband? Weapons? Somehow, she didn't think so.

Mainly, she wanted to hear him speak his own language. A Muscovite, definitely, and educated, but his business was in St. Petersburg.

He continued talking and asked if they could meet the next day for tea and to discuss the possibility of her working for him. He suggested about four thirty at the Palm Court of the Plaza Hotel. She almost laughed. The Palm Court of the Plaza! She instantly had a vision of a man and woman discussing high-powered business affairs amid tables of aging tourists, matrons from Scarsdale, and mothers with overdressed children.

But she agreed.

After she hung up the phone, Elena remained motionless, staring at the instrument, which had brought this voice into her life. It was not the offer of the job or the money that interested her. She was perfectly content to live modestly on the retirement income she and Clarke had planned to live on together. She cherished the time she now had to spend with Katya and Sascha. It was the man's voice, deep and, she thought, familiar—a voice she had not heard in almost thirty years.

So, here she was on the subway on her way to tea at the Plaza. She was aware of a stab of fear somewhere near her solar plexus. It reminded her of that last day in Berlin, but then everything since yesterday reminded her of that day.

She was nineteen then and dancing with the Kirov. She was a native of Leningrad; the Kirov had been her life, from earliest school days when she showed talent. At sixteen, she was asked to join the *corps de ballet* and that last night in East Berlin she danced a *pas de quatre* in *Swan Lake*.

Hungry, as she always was after a performance, she had promised earlier to join a distant cousin and his friends for a late supper. Her cousin, Russian by birth, had worked in East Germany for more than five years. Ivan had taken its German equivalent, Johann, as his name. She must remember to call him that in front of his friends. She anticipated a supper—perhaps meager but made jolly by young company, perhaps many originally from Russia—and plenty of wine and vodka.

"You were stupendous!" Johann said when she met him outside the dressing room.

"Well, perhaps at least good." She laughed.

"Let me take your bag," he said, indicating the bulky canvas shoulder bag she carried.

"No, no," she demurred. The bag was neither light nor heavy, but contained her precious shoes, stage makeup, passport and documents, and the cross her mother had given her when she was twelve. She put the bag on the floor, unzipped it, and fished in it for the cross. She slipped it around her neck, dropping it inside her sweater. She also pulled out a pair of white kid gloves. They looked awkward with her rough coat, but she had lost her winter gloves at the last stop on the tour and had only these white ones she had brought along for the few formal occasions when the troupe was entertained somewhere.

She slipped on her coat, and they went out into the damp night. As they crossed a park, away from any pedestrians, Johann stopped and turned her to face him.

"Where would you rather dance than anywhere in the world?" he asked in a hushed voice.

Startled at the abrupt question, she gaped at him for a moment and then stammered, "In America." To Elena, her voice sounded choked. She had never said that aloud before, even to herself.

Johann's expression did not change. "Tonight, I will give you the chance," he said in a dramatic whisper.

"What?" Surely he was joking.

"Tonight, Elena, three friends of mine and I will cross over. Do you want to go with us?"

"But…" She hesitated. Her first thought was that in less than two hours, she really should be back at the hotel where the troupe was staying. They were to leave Berlin at 5:00 in the morning, and the wake-up call would come early. She was stunned by the thought that by 5:00 her entire life could be changed. She temporized. "But there are no arrangements."

"But there are," he said. "The people on the other side are expecting four men and a woman. There are papers, air tickets, everything."

"For me?"

"No, actually. A woman friend of ours was to go, but she got cold feet at the last moment. Say you'll take her place. Elena, you should dance for the world!"

Elena looked at his outline, the only thing she could see in the dark. Johann was always so dramatic. A chill ran through her. This was too soon. This was too haphazard. Yet again, this might be her only chance.

Still, she hesitated.

"What are you leaving behind? Nothing you can't do without. Don't you have everything you really need in that bag?" Johann patted the canvas bag she was clutching.

"I will think," she said. "I will think."

He took her arm and they walked on through the deserted streets to a house. Johann had a key that opened the front door. Perhaps he was also the key to her future, she thought.

Instead of the supper she was expecting, she found herself in a cramped apartment with her cousin and three other young men. Dinner was going to consist of stale bread, old cheese, and half a bottle of cheap vodka.

One of the men scowled at her cousin and remarked in German, "You're crazy to bring her here."

"Let her decide," said Johann.

The man sneered and looked away, angry.

One of the other men bit his fingernails. He looked white. "I tell you, she has betrayed us."

Elena wondered if they were talking about her or about the woman whose place she might take.

"No way would she do that," said the third man. "She is just afraid. I know my wife. She would never betray me. She just wants me to go first and take a chance on joining me later. To tell you the truth, I am happier about that arrangement myself." He swirled a glass of vodka as he talked, took a sip, and put the glass on the table with a gesture of finality.

"So," said the angry man, turning to Elena, "are you game to go with us?"

She was startled to hear her voice say in German, "*Ja.*"

Her German was decent, if not exactly fluent. Her head began to ache with the effort of understanding all they were telling her. They explained that they would go separately to the house where there was a tunnel to the western section of Berlin. The angry man would go first, then the frightened one, and then the husband. Elena and Johann would be last.

She struggled to memorize the directions. They did not have much time. Within half an hour, she found herself walking alone on the streets of the city. She was afraid of the dark but more afraid of the streets she would have to maneuver when she was closer to the wall, which was brightly lit. She slung her canvas bag across her chest so that she could hide her hands with the white gloves in her pocket.

She followed their instructions, working her way close to the *Strasse* she would take to the house. Then she thought she had taken a wrong turn. She doubled back a little and, with relief, made out the street sign she was looking for. Now it was only a matter of working her way in the shadows of the dilapidated houses to number Eighty-Nine. She caught sight of number Seventy-Six and began to count: Seventy-Seven, Seventy-Nine, Eighty-One. In her hurry and her consternation, she pulled her hands out of her pockets and shifted the canvas bag, remembering then to hide the reflective gloves in her pockets once more.

The number "83" was worn but visible on the next door frame. She walked faster. Eighty-Five, Eighty-Seven, she counted, and then she saw him.

He was a big man in a long dark coat and hat. He was standing in the doorway of number Eighty-Seven, and she could smell KGB. She stopped, immobilized as a deer aware of the odor of a hunter too close. She poised to run.

"Elena Yvgenskaya." His voice was as deep as the night that prevented her from seeing his face. "You danced beautifully tonight."

She felt her heart and soul drop like a stone. What had she done? She should be back at the hotel this moment.

He moved languidly and took her arm. He opened the door of number Eighty-Seven, pulled her into an unlit hall, opened the first door on her left, and closed the door behind them.

"Listen to me," he said. "Don't make a sound. There is nothing, I repeat, nothing you can do to affect what will take place in the next half hour. Stay here. Stay out of sight. Make no sign to anyone. I will come later and take you back to the hotel." His Russian was excellent. The deep voice held just a hint of the Muscovite.

He opened the door and added, "I will also lock the door."

The scrape of the key in the lock was almost welcome. Her relief and her fear were so equal they canceled each other out. The only thing she knew was she had to urinate. Luckily the room had a water closet.

She looked around. In the dim light coming through the blinds from the street, she could see a bed, dresser, and a small chair. She put her bag on the floor and used the bathroom. Just as she came back into the room, she saw the shadows of a man's head and shoulders pass the window. It could have been Johann, or it could have been the tall man.

She reached the window in time to hear the first singsong, singsong, singsong of police vehicles. Their blue lights slashed through the slats of the blinds. She pressed herself against the corner of the wall and opened the blinds just enough to see something of what was going on in the street. There were policemen everywhere. The tall man had his back to her and was standing next to another man in a dark coat. She watched as the *polizei* loaded four handcuffed men into a van. The frightened man was first, then the husband, then Johann, and the last was the angry man, who put up a struggle. A policeman hit him over the head several times. The blood looked red in the light and black in the shadows.

One by one, the vehicles pulled away, leaving the street again quiet and dark, deserted by everyone except the two men in their long coats. They approached the window where Elena stood. She could hear most of their conversation, their heads at the level of her waist. They spoke in Russian.

The shorter man spoke. "Get some sleep, Gregor. I'll go stay at the tunnel until they come in the morning to brick it up. The girl may show yet."

"I don't think so," said the tall man. "I think it was just happenstance she visited her cousin tonight. She may already be back at the hotel with the troupe." Then he added, "But it is best to be careful. Good night, comrade."

The short man pushed away from the wall under her window and walked toward number Eighty-Nine. The tall man waited a moment and then turned from the window. She heard the door in the hall open and close, then the scratch of the key. She continued to press against the wall.

He closed the door and leaned against it.

"So," he said, "you will return to the ballet?"

"Yes. Please. If you can arrange it."

"I can," he said, "but there is a price."

She frowned in the dark and did not answer.

"As soon as I make love to you, I will take you back to the hotel, explaining you got lost on your way to the hotel from supper with your cousin."

She gasped at the implication of what he said. Well, she thought, so be it. She was not a virgin and her few sexual encounters had been brief and unsatisfactory. This could be no worse, and it would all be over soon. Poor Johann. But she could not do anything for him.

"All right"

She pulled off the white gloves, stuffed them in the pocket of her coat, and took off the coat, dropping it across the small chair. The room was cold, but she was methodical. Next came her sweater and blouse, then the wool skirt, the long, thick stockings, and last her underwear. The room was dark, and she was glad, not because she was modest but because her underthings were so shabby. The only thing she did not remove was the cross on its gold chain. She quickly slipped under the blankets on the bed. The sheets smelled musty with the sharp odor of cotton, not necessarily dirty but long unwashed.

The tall man stood motionless as she undressed, but once she was in bed he began an identical ritual. She was surprised from what she could see that he was a big man, but not fat, only well muscled. He was also obviously ready for intercourse. This shouldn't take long.

He got into the bed next to her, and she was grateful for the body heat. His movements were no more hurried than they had been from the moment she saw him at the doorway. Curiously, instead of touching her, he lifted the cross to his lips in a solemn gesture.

My God, she thought, what is he expecting, a religious experience?

He began by barely touching her with his fingertips and surprised her with a long and gentle kiss. From that moment, she lost track of time. She was completely absorbed by the feelings he aroused, feelings she had experienced in fantasy or just before the rude reality of the sexual encounters she had experienced, but never during the act.

Finally he entered her, and she came almost immediately. Her orgasm seemed to surprise him. It astounded her.

When he was finished, he held her a moment, then without getting out of bed, pulled open the drawer of the dresser and produced a bottle of vodka, some bread, and cheese, considerably better and fresher than those she had shared with the Germans. The food and drink were welcome, but all she wanted to do was sleep. She was also aware that she didn't want to leave the bed or him.

"I suppose we should go," she said.

"We can wait if you wish, so long as we are gone from here by the time the men get here to brick up the tunnel. The street will then be full of people."

"The troupe leaves at 5:00 in the morning."

"Then sleep a little. I will wake you in time. Then when I make your excuses, the *maître de ballet* will perhaps be too busy to be angry with you."

She didn't argue. She was already asleep.

He roused her shortly after 4:00 with a kiss, and she responded by putting her arms around him.

"I suppose we don't have time for this," she said.

His reply was a non sequitur. "I saw you dance in Stalingrad, when you were just a little girl, and I have been watching you ever since. You are very good, you know. You will do well. Already you have been singled out from the corps." He was silent a moment and then added, "You would have a better chance to star in America, you think?"

"I am told they love Russian dancers. Certainly the men have done well. I don't know."

He sat up and pulled her into a sitting position facing him. He took her face in his hands and looked directly at her. The dim light from the blinds gave her the best view of him yet: square jaw, high cheekbones, and dark eyes.

"Elena," he said, "you must decide. You go or you stay. If you stay, we will go back now to the hotel. If you go, I think I can get my comrade to leave the house next door for coffee shortly before the men arrive to do the work. You will have only a few minutes between then and when they come to brick up the tunnel. What is your decision?"

"When would I go?"

"In about an hour."

"I will go."

Today, riding the subway in New York, Elena smiled. She still wondered how much of her decision had been about dance and how much had been about another hour with the tall man. It was an hour well spent. In twenty minutes, they had accomplished everything either of them could ever want. The word "efficient" crossed her mind, and she nearly laughed aloud.

Each of them dressed and unselfconsciously used the water closet. By a few minutes before 5:00, they were in their coats, and Elena began to pull on the white gloves.

"For God's sake, not those," he said. "I saw you coming a kilometer away." He took the gloves and stuffed them into his own pocket. Then he handed her his own large black ones. "Wear these."

"Surely, I don't need them just to go next door."

"Skin reflects too. Pull your scarf forward to hide your face."

He nodded his good-bye, when what she wanted was for him to take her in his arms just once more. Then he was gone. The shadow of his hat passed the window.

She waited and waited. Despair began to make her breath come more quickly. She had now given up all chance of joining the troupe before it left. At a quarter to six, she heard voices. They came from her right. The two men passed the window, the tall man, hatless, his dark hair shining in the first light, walked with his arm around his comrade's shoulders. They were laughing.

Elena quickly left the room. She waited until their footsteps faded and slipped out of the door as though opening it too far would alert the neighborhood. Actually, most of the houses in this district close to the wall appeared unoccupied, derelict. By now, there should be other people on the street. Perhaps people did not want to live so close to the wall, or they were removed from their homes. She had no trouble reaching the other door undetected.

She hurried down the hall and to the basement of the building. At the bottom of the stairs was a room with a boiler and other equipment. On a small table was a magazine, a thermos bottle, and a man's cap, along with the hat the tall man had been wearing earlier. She slipped off the gloves he had given her and laid them under the hat, so that the man with him would not notice, but Gregor would know she had escaped.

She pushed the canvas bag into the hole and got down on her hands and knees to crawl through the tunnel, pushing the bag ahead of her. She could hear scuffling and voices in the upper hall. Terrified, she pushed and crawled, afraid the men would hear her efforts. Would they follow her into the tunnel?

The passage was totally dark, damp, and gritty once she was past the foundation of the house. She scraped along. Her breath sounded loud and raspy in the closed space. She began to feel claustrophobic, but she pushed and crawled, unable to see anything ahead of her and with no idea how long the passage was.

She began to think it would never end and she would die of exhaustion in the hole when the canvas bag suddenly dropped from sight, exposing the end of the tunnel. The bag dropped to the concrete floor of a basement with a thud, surprising a man standing a few feet away.

"What's this?" he said in German. "*Fraulein*! You made it. We thought everyone was arrested. Are you the dancer?"

She could only nod.

He led her to a small lavatory where she could scrub the dirt from her hands and nails. She washed her face and brushed as much of the soil from her hair as she could, tying back her long hair. She could do little about her muddy stockings and coat, but she shook off what she could.

When she was finished, he said they would take her for coffee and bread.

The café where they took her was warm and welcoming. The man bought huge cups of coffee and sweet breads. He had not questioned her too closely, but now he was all curiosity. How had she managed to escape?

She wanted to lie, but whatever inventiveness she possessed was lost in a brain she was afraid had quit functioning entirely.

"I got lost," she said. "Then I found the house."

"Was this after they arrested the others?"

"Yes. I hid and watched the *polizei*."

"You must have been terrified."

"I was."

He smoked his cigarette and looked at her through the smoke with narrowed eyes. "It is very odd they would not leave someone on watch to see if you came later. Also, where did you hide?"

"In the house next door." She was obviously trying to give as little information as possible.

"In the house next door?" he repeated. "Was there no one there?"

"Yes. A man. He helped me."

"A man helped you in that house? What did he look like?"

She started to make up a description, but just shrugged. "It was dark. There were no lights."

"A man helped you. A big man? Tall? With dark hair and eyes."

She betrayed herself with a surprised look at her interrogator.

"*Der Hammer?*" he said in awe.

"The what?"

"The 'Hammer,' Gregor Kalnikov. He's KGB—very good." The man looked at her speculatively. "Why would he do that? What did he say to you?" His tone was speculative, as though he was talking to himself.

"He said he had seen me dance."

"Seen you dance?" he asked. Elena blushed at the incredulity in his voice and her own memories.

A half smile came to the face of the German. Cigarette smoke made pirouettes from the corner of his mouth. His eyes were amused. "And we all thought he was the exception to prove the rule."

"Rule?"

"Gregor the incorruptible, Gregor the heartless,—so he is human after all." He laughed a low knowing laugh, and Elena nearly choked on her coffee. She hoped the cup hid her face.

The next twelve weeks were a dream and a nightmare. The man produced papers for her and took her to the American Embassy. She was questioned by the CIA officers there and finally escorted to a plane bound for Frankfurt and New York City. The American Embassy saw to it that the proper people were notified in the ballet world of New York, so when she arrived, representatives of the American Ballet Theatre greeted her. She danced for them, danced for them again, and was told to report to rehearsals. On the third day of rehearsal, perhaps because she was trying too hard, perhaps because she did not feel well, she fell. She broke her ankle.

The people from the company took her to an orthopedist, a Dr. Miller. He X-rayed her leg, set the broken bones, and put her in a cast. Then he told her he had done all he could do for her and that the break was so severe she would probably never dance professionally again.

She sat in the waiting room when he was finished. She wanted to cry but could not. She was terrified. How would she earn a living? What would she do? Suicide, perhaps? But no, in the circumstances, that was impossible.

By the greatest chance, or perhaps a miracle, Dr. Miller had a brother who was a balletomane, and he happened to drop by the office. This was Clarke, who had been in his brother's office as Elena was being treated.

He came into the waiting room, introduced himself, and began to talk to Elena. He was deeply impressed that she had danced with the Kirov. He was kind, and his sympathy brought forth the tears she was harboring. Soon she was crying hysterically in his arms, and the rest, as Americans say, is history.

By this time in her ruminations, Elena was walking down Fifty-Ninth Street from the Lexington Avenue stop toward the Plaza. She crossed Fifth Avenue and entered the hotel. The dim lobby seemed bright compared to the gloomy weather.

As she approached the Palm Court, she saw him. He had his back, still trim and square shouldered, to her; she noticed the fine cut and cloth of his dark suit. English tailoring, she thought. Definitely London. His dark hair was now a steel gray. The voice was the same.

"There is not a lady here waiting? I am late."

The hostess shook her head.

"Mr. Ulanov?"

He turned and relief showed on his face. The square jaw had softened some with age. The eyes were dark as chocolate with deep red lights that sparkled when he was animated. Elena realized this was the first time she had seen him in full light.

"Mrs. Miller," he said. It was a statement, not a question, and his eyes flicked ever so briefly at the gold cross around her neck.

"Yes." They shook hands in the European manner.

They sat at a small table over tea and pastries. She suddenly longed for a good glass of Russian tea, instead of the strange, anemic American brew she never quite got used to, and wished he had suggested the Russian Tea Room instead. He asked about her family, expressed his sympathy for Clarke's death, and generally let her know there was little he did not know about her. He explained again the circumstances surrounding his fledgling business.

She listened patiently, nibbled at the pastry, and finally sat with her hands folded in her lap. She heard him and understood, but was also aware that the attraction to him had never waned. She would wait to see how this played out.

"Mrs. Miller, are you at all interested in my business proposition?" he finally asked bluntly.

"Yes, Mr. Ulanov, I am," she said simply.

He hesitated. "Then there is something more you should know," he said. He put his hand in the pocket of the elegant suit and pulled out a pair of white kid gloves. He laid them on the table between them. Elena noticed they had yellowed slightly with age. She did not respond, and he seemed unable to look at her.

Finally, he looked up and said, "Perhaps you do not remember your gloves?"

"Oh, I remember," she said. "I thought your name was Gregor Kalnikov."

He shrugged, masking any surprise he felt at her knowledge. "My passport and all of my papers say I am Micha Ulanov. So I suppose that is who I am."

"Did you know the Germans called you *der Hammer?*"

"Elena." He leaned his crossed forearms on the table, his face earnest in its entreaty. "Is it possible for you to forget the past? If you blame me for what happened, I ask your forgiveness, although I had an impression you were as pleased with things as I was."

At this, she smiled and reached for her purse.

"You wish to go?"

"No, no," she said in an offhand way. She pulled her wallet from her purse.

"Please, I will pay."

"No, no, no!" she said more emphatically.

She opened the wallet to the picture section. There was Tanya, smiling her father's smile, her arms around two of the South African women with whom she worked. Next was a picture of her son and his family, his pretty wife, blond daughter, and solemn son. He stood behind them, tall, square shouldered with dark hair and eyes the color of chocolate that glowed with red lights when he was excited.

She removed the picture, turned it to face her companion, and laid it on top of the white kid gloves.

CHRISTMAS LIST

When Kevin Clark looked in the mirror that morning, he saw a slim man in his thirties, slightly sallow but clear eyed. He was neat and clean shaven, but he did not look happy.

In less than an hour, he would age fifty years and have a long white beard and a paunch. He would also be dressed in a red velvet Santa Claus suit provided to him by a large mall near Newburgh. Joe Manners, who at the moment was driving the two of them to work, found him the job. Kevin knew he should be grateful, but he still was not happy.

The roadside along the Taconic was cheerless. Tufts of dirty snow lay among the trees and brambles like bits of paper towel on the floor of a public bathroom. The sky was heavy but without the promise of more snow or, to Kevin's eyes, anything else.

"Hey, buddy, you're glum today." Joe's voice was always cheery on these morning drives, a subject of wonder to Kevin. "What's the matter, the little darlings getting to you?"

"Not really."

"They can be great, and they can be a pain in the ass—as can the parents." Joe was also a Santa Claus in a smaller mall north of the one he was taking Kevin to. This was the fourth Christmas season Joe had played Santa to the children at the mall.

Kevin didn't answer. He didn't want to talk shop. He didn't want to talk sports either, the usual subject on the morning drives.

Joe's voice took on a slightly more serious tone. "What's eatin' you, Kevin?"

After a pause, he continued, "You have a job, you get paid, you get your driver's license back in three weeks, and you haven't had a drink in almost six months. Have you?"

At the final question, Joe gave Kevin a quick, hard look and then concentrated on the road.

"No. It's just…" He paused. "It's nothin'."

"Nothin's always somethin'. Out with it." There was a note of command here.

"Every day, I'm scared I'm going to look up from ho, ho, ho-ing and there will be Andrea with Jason. At first I was really scared, and as the weeks went by I thought the chance of that happening was silly, and I relaxed a little. But the last couple of days I've been edgy as a rottweiler."

"Look, we've talked about this. It's her mother that lives close to the mall. She'll probably take the kid to a Santa someplace closer to Peekskill. Even if she does, with all that stuff on, Jason won't recognize you, and neither will she."

"I'm just afraid I would freeze and start crying with Jason on my lap or say something where she'll recognize me."

"And what would she do, call the cops?"

"You don't know Andrea. She might. She might even wave the restraining order in my face. Can't you see the headline, 'Estranged Wife Attacks Santa in Local Mall'?"

"Gee, Kevin, somehow I don't think so." Joe's chuckle irritated Kevin, but Joe went on more seriously. "Now Jason is another matter. You know what our training tells us; we have to really listen and be sensitive to what the kids want. In your case, just keep Jason and his welfare in the front of your mind. The good Lord will carry you through."

Joe stopped the car at the entrance to the mall and turned to face Kevin. The older man gave Kevin a squeeze on the forearm. "Take care, Kevin. It's going to be fine."

Kevin only nodded and swung himself out of the rider's side of the pickup. He reached over the back seat and pulled out the small duffel bag that made him look like he was on his way to the gym. Instead of slimming down, he was about to put on fifty pounds. He smiled at the thought and saw Joe's face relax a little. The horn tooted once, lightly, as the truck pulled away, taking Joe to his own place of transformation.

Behind the management office in the mall was a room where employees could rest and leave their belongings in lockers. This was where Kevin became Santa Claus. The only person in the office when he went in was Jennie, the receptionist.

"Hi, Kevin," she said, and without waiting for his answering greeting rushed on, "the real Santa got here before you!" She pushed across the desk a box containing the newest Lego blocks that assembled into replicas of an action film Jason loved. The sets were hard to find, and Jennie dated one of the guys who worked in the mall toy store.

"Jennie, you're wonderful. Thanks so much!" he said, and was genuinely touched she had taken the trouble to get the toy for him. "This will make Christmas for Jason."

"No problem," she said. "Glad to do it."

Kevin took the box into the lounge and began the laborious process of turning a thirty-two-year-old, 170-pound man into Santa Claus. The clothes and padding were not uncomfortable, just bulky and hot. Actually, he loved the feel of the fine red velvet and the white fur. It brought back memories of his own childhood pilgrimages to see Santa and ask for the precious gifts.

He thought about the Lego set and its importance to Jason. Kevin wished his own desires were as simple, instead of the deep desire to regain a lost, or at least distant, child.

He hated the spirit gum and all the mess of attaching the false beard. Finally, he put on the hat, and all that was left of Kevin was a pair of startling blue eyes.

The padding made him waddle slightly. He locked up his wallet and clothes and started for the atrium of the mall, where he had a huge carved chair waiting for him. It was set in what he thought was a rather hokey stage set with plastic elves and a wooden cottage not much better than a Potemkin village.

The children were already lining up. This was it, even if he needed to use the bathroom, until the noon break. He carefully set the hands of a wooden clock decorated with holly to indicate Santa would be at his post until twelve o'clock.

Then began the only part of the job he really liked. That was talking to the children. Well, he mused, in essence that *was* the job, so maybe he was lucky.

But it was tiring. He could see the mall clock that recorded real time, and by 11:50, he was ready for his break. Then he saw them over the head of a blond six-year-old girl. Andrea wore a long camel-colored coat. He knew her silky red hair came from a bottle, but he always liked it. Jason was wearing a red car coat with a hood and jeans, his standard outfit. Kevin lost his concentration, and the child on his lap was looking at him curiously. A few steps away, her mother was frowning.

"I'm sorry, sweetie," he said. "Santa's getting old and his mind wanders. What did you say?" The little girl giggled and repeated her request. The mother was smiling again.

The obligatory picture was taken, and the child climbed down from his lap, secure in the impression that all her desires would be fulfilled.

I wish, thought Kevin.

Then there was Jason. Kevin deepened his voice and affected a drawl. "So, sonny, do you want to sit on Santa's lap and tell him what's on your Christmas list?"

Jason nodded shyly, not looking at his face. Kevin helped the boy up on his lap. The child's smell was achingly familiar. He stole a look at Andrea. Her mouth was slightly agape, and there was a tiny frown between her eyes. When she saw his eyes, her face set in a grim line of recognition.

Oh shit, he thought.

He started the familiar routine with Jason, asking about the list. Jason repeated a number of things, including the Lego set. When he got to that, Kevin looked Andrea full in the face and gave a very slight nod. She raised her eyebrows to acknowledge the signal. When he wasn't drinking, communication had never been one of their problems.

Jason was hesitating. "Anything else?"

"Yes," the child whispered.

"What's that?" Kevin prompted

The child buried his head in the white beard and lowered his voice. Kevin knew that Andrea had heard the whispered request anyway. "I want my dad home for Christmas."

Kevin could feel the tears. God, he couldn't cry now. He couldn't let Jason know, even if the child had a vague suspicion that he wasn't Santa.

"Well," he said slowly, "I can't promise that. But maybe if you ask your mother—nicely—maybe Christmas day your dad could visit. Will you do that? Will you ask Mom?"

The child nodded, not looking up. They both smiled for the camera.

He watched as Jason took Andrea's hand. They walked on a few steps, and the boy turned to wave good-bye. Kevin didn't think he really recognized his father, but he wasn't sure. Jason seemed content and turned to walk on.

Andrea stared a long time at him and then gave a decisive nod. Kevin mentally put a big check mark by the item at the top of his personal Christmas list.

BE CAREFUL WHAT YOU WISH FOR

For the thousandth time, she bit back the urge to say, "God, Mother, get rid of that thing!" She had said it once, thirty years ago, and once was enough.

The kitchen window faced south, husbanding a few of the available winter rays of sun. They slanted across the worn blue and white squares of asbestos tile and plaster wall, where the sunbeams arranged themselves geometrically in neat parallelograms formed by the wide slats of clean venetian blinds.

Six of the bars fell across a wall calendar hung from a nail painted over by the same paint as the wall until it resembled a tiny mushroom. The paint in the kitchen was new and still smelled slightly of latex. The picture on the calendar curled down at the corners like a frown. Where the light hit it, the broken color reproduction of the Childe Hassam painting resembled the confetti of a ticker tape parade, and the scene was Fifth Avenue, crowded and hung with a rank of American flags. The date was July 1967.

Carole Feldstein glanced at the calendar, moved her chair so that she faced the window more directly than the wall, and pushed a half-full coffee cup and saucer away from in front of her to an empty place on the round table so that she could open the black carryall wallet. Today, the zipper decided to be contrary, and she found herself jerking at it in frustration until the sound of its opening ripped the air. She flipped it open until one of the double plastic compartments revealed a current calendar. The other compartment held a picture of two children, a boy of eight and a girl of ten.

"Mother, are you listening?" She hoped her voice held enough urgency to get attention and yet hide her impatience.

The frail woman on the other side of the table picked at a napkin, stretching the edges into an irregular scallop. Her concentration was as intent as a child's with a coloring book.

Carole took a spiral notebook from the top of a stack of catalogues on the counter, well within arms' reach in the tiny apartment kitchen. The notebook looked almost as well worn as the calendar but was considerably newer. It contained information printed in large block letters.

There were columns for the days of the week and names of medications inserted meticulously below each of them. The number of pills and the hour they should be taken each day were highlighted, with the number in blue and the hour in yellow.

Some of the entries had wobbly checkmarks beside them. Some did not.

Carole counted the checkmarks. This week there were fewer of them than entries, but that did not necessarily mean the medication had been ignored. It might mean her mother simply had forgotten to check off the dose taken.

She sighed. She had tried everything. First, she bought the pink plastic box with a compartment for each day of the week. Her mother couldn't open the box.

Luckily, other than vitamins, there were not a great number of pills that absolutely had to be taken by the older woman. But at least one of them, her heart medication, was crucial to her health and could not be skipped. The doctor had been especially emphatic about this. So what was Carole to do? She finally resorted to lining up the bottles, making out the schedule and calling her mother each day to see if the proper medication had been taken.

On Sundays, Carole came out to Howard Beach for her filial visit and to check on the medication. Usually, the contents of the bottles had been ingested imperfectly. This week, to Carole's relief, the heart medicine was all gone. She only hoped it had disappeared down her mother's throat and had not been misplaced or thrown away. This was becoming a matter of trusting that some supreme power would look out for things.

This sort of trust was not in Carole's makeup. She had gone into the mental health care field partly because she wanted to serve people, partly because it was both foreign and close to what her father did, and partly because she loved to have things orderly and neat around her. Other people's messiness and wastefulness irked her.

Her mind went back to the calendar.

"I see you hung the calendar up again after management painted," she said.

Her mother just nodded.

"Why, Mother? Why?"

"You know why: because your father liked it."

Carol wanted to retort, "But you hated him." Instead she said, "I've never understood if you liked it yourself, kept it as a memorial, or maybe just liked looking at it to celebrate how long he's been gone."

Her mother did not answer but shrugged her narrow shoulders dismissively and asked, "How are the kids?"

"They're okay. I always worry about them the weekends they're with Ben."

"He's a good dad."

"But he doesn't watch them the way I do."

Her mother's mouth seemed to curl in a sly smile. Carole caught the fleeting expression.

"I just want them to be safe, Mom. That's all."

"Sure."

"What do you mean sure? Sure like of course, or sure like don't give me that?"

"Of course like of course."

What Carole did not tell her mother was that the children, more each week, seemed to prefer their rather laissez-faire father to Carole's stricter discipline. Naturally, she thought, naturally, but boundaries had to be kept. She wanted to be sure her children became responsible adults, not like her brother, Keith, and she felt her influence on them slipping subtly. She was terrified.

"Has Keith called lately?" she asked her mother.

"Yesterday. He's fine."

"What did he have to say for himself?"

"Not much. He's still working at the health food store. He mostly wanted to see how I was feeling."

"I suppose he pitched you on some homeopathic medicine again?"

"We talked a little about it."

"What was he recommending?"

"A number of things; I didn't pay too much attention."

Carole had the feeling her mother was hiding something. "I'll fix us some lunch," she said.

The refrigerator was full of bits of this and that. Carole began to check expiration dates and toss some things in the tall garbage can next to the sink. She was unaware that she had her "no nonsense" expression on her face—a frown between her dark eyes—but her mother, still shredding what was left of the napkin, kept glancing at her.

"Do you want some cottage cheese?" Carole asked. "It's just about to go bad." She put the carton on the drain board next to the sink and started to throw out a package of Swiss cheese.

"Don't throw that away," her mother said, her voice sharp if not authoritative.

"It's moldy."

"I don't care."

"Have it your way." Carol started to replace the cheese in the drawer when she saw the bottle, hidden behind a jar of grape jam in the door of the refrigerator. She picked it up and recognized it as an herbal remedy, reputed to help heart ailments.

"Mom, you're not taking this stuff, are you?"

"Keith says it's fine and won't hurt me."

"He's not a doctor."

"Well, neither are you. That kind of doctor."

"For God's sake, Mother, didn't you learn anything from living with my father? He was 'that kind' of doctor, and you know how he felt about quacks and quack medicine."

"He was a quack."

"He was not a quack. He was a fine internist and made a real difference in people's lives."

"Well, he certainly made a difference in that Horton woman's life."

Carole swallowed her anger and concentrated on placing servings of peach and cottage cheese on two plates. There was enough bread and turkey breast for sandwiches, but she would have to go to the grocery store before she had enough food for an evening meal for the two of them. Shopping and laundry were part of her weekly routine here, and she supposed she should be grateful her mother was still able to live alone. There certainly was no room for her in the tiny Manhattan apartment Carole and the children shared.

She felt a flash of resentment as she buttered the bread. Mother *would* bring up the Horton affair. It was the malpractice suit over her father's care of the indigent woman that eventually led to his suicide, which left his family in relatively straitened circumstances. Carole and her mother had both worked to see Carole through high school, college, and graduate school.

Regardless of her mother's remark, Carole was inordinately proud of her PhD. She knew her mother would have worked just as hard to put Keith through school, but he preferred to follow what he called an alternative lifestyle. Certainly, he never wanted to be any sort of doctor. But her mother's insistence on bringing up the Horton affair nettled Carole. Her father had made a difference in people's lives. He had been, if not a great doctor, at least competent, or so she thought. A niggling doubt about his abilities and her own competence jostled with lingering feelings of hostility. To make a difference: that was all she had wanted to do—to help fix people, and perhaps not to have another Horton thing happen.

She dropped the knife, took the bottle of herbal medicine, and poured it down the garbage disposal.

"What are you doing?" her mother screeched.

"You've taken half of this, and you haven't asked your doctor if you could. Have you?"

Her mother looked away and sat down again at the table from which she had gotten up, as if to do battle at last with her daughter.

Carole just stared at her mother and went to the telephone in the hallway. She dialed the area code and a number in California.

A generic message on the answering machine clicked on. How strange, she thought, that her way-out brother should have a generic message. At the tone, she began in a quiet, almost sultry voice. "If you don't pay attention to me and stop fooling around with her, I'm going to catch a plane to California. I mean it this time, I've had enough. I'll call you back when we can talk specifics." She banged down the phone and went back to the kitchen.

The action she had taken turned all the anger into self-pity, and she kept repeating to herself, "All I wanted to do was make a difference in somebody's life."

A continent away during the evening hours, a telephone in a San Francisco apartment showed the New York number on its caller identification. The number had "unavailable" below it where the name of the calling party was usually listed.

The telephone was not in the apartment of Carole's brother. She had misdialed. By mere coincidence, the telephone was in the townhouse of a rather fragile young woman named Janice. She had suspected for some time that her live-in lover, who often flew to New York, had another interest. She played the message over and over again while drinking Scotch on the rocks.

When her lover came through the door, she shot him five times with the .38 pistol he kept in his bedside drawer. She reserved the last bullet for her own head.

THE SOUND OF BRASS
CYMBALS

He stood just beyond the tinted-glass window, clearly visible to the five of us sitting in the ship's lounge. His face was long and square jawed, the curly hair gray and thin at the temples, and the long Semitic nose curved above a sweet and somewhat diffident smile. Tall and still lithe at sixty, he was neatly dressed in khaki pants and a shirt with buttoned tabs at the shoulders.

The boys crowded in front of him, gesturing, excited, their slender bodies covered by the pale colors of the traditional Egyptian *djallabahs*, tight across the arms and torso, then flaring elegantly from pleats at the hip. He was a Jew, and they were Arabs, and the bargaining was intense. We could not hear the words, but the man gestured toward a string of turquoise beads. His left arm was already loaded with strings of glass beads of all colors. He and a boy of ten or twelve struck a deal and exchanged dirty, crumpled bank notes for the offered treasure.

"There goes Sol again. He does this at every stop. It's amazing," said the man in the polo shirt.

"This is the last stop. I wonder what he'll do with all that junk?" asked the Polo Shirt's wife. She was an avid golfer and wore matching shorts and shirt emblazoned with a country club logo. They had names, John and Susan, but my husband always referred to them in private as "the Polo Shirt" and "Ms. County Club."

Sol's wife smiled a vacant smile and tugged at the thong of her sandal. She was a second wife, blond and gentile.

My husband sat up and hitched at his blue blazer. "I don't know," he said. "You know what he's been doing? He buys the stuff at one stop, gives it all away to the kids when we get to the next stop on the river, and buys some more." Four heads nodded at this recapitulation. I did not respond. My attention was solely on the scene between the man, and the boys.

The Etape Hotel sat solidly beyond the quay and street behind the man. Out of sight to the right were the temples of Luxor and Karnak. To the left was the museum we had visited that morning, full of silent masks, effigies, and mummies. Behind us, across the Nile, lay the sand-covered tombs, the City of the Dead.

We were scheduled to fly from Luxor to Cairo in the afternoon and, ready to debark, luggage was piled around us. The conversation weighed on me as heavily as the overstuffed baggage. My hands curled over the pale upholstered arms of the chair, inert. My body was overcome by an almost catatonic lethargy. Something about the quiet opulence of the lounge separated by two layers of glass from the noisy smells and sights of Luxor, all in the presence of such antiquity, depressed me.

In the sun, sweat glistened along Sol's hairline. He was laughing. He took the ropes of glass from his left arm and began to toss them to the boys, haphazardly, the way crews toss plastic beads to revelers from floats in the New Orleans parade at Mardi Gras. A spectrum of colors caught the light. The boys scrambled and jostled each other to retrieve the booty.

"Well, I'll be damned," said the Polo Shirt.

"Well, John, I guess we ought to go give Hassan his *baksheesh*," said my husband, losing interest in the action beyond the window.

"I'll go with you. I want to tell him good-bye," said Ms. Country Club.

The three of them stood, pulling together whatever was left of the Egyptian money. The two men compared notes on an appropriate amount for the tip and began to move toward the door of the lounge. Sol's wife pulled her wallet from her purse and rose to join them, her eyes at once bright and vacant. I wondered if she was on Valium.

Earlier that day I had bid Hassan, our guide, good-bye, given him some US "greenbacks," and thanked him not only for his care but also for his skill in settling a particularly nasty argument among the bus drivers on one of the excursions. He surprised me by kissing me ceremonially on both cheeks.

Sol came in the door just as the party reached it.

"Craziest thing I've ever seen," said the Polo Shirt, clapping Sol on the shoulder.

"I was afraid you were going to be loaded down with all that junk," said Ms. Country Club. "Then you just gave it all away."

"Good thing!" joked my husband. "I didn't see how you were going to get it on the airplane. Probably be overweight." The three of them exited laughing, followed by Sol's still smiling, still wordless wife.

Sol folded his long body into the chair next to me.

We both stared out the window at the pedestrians and horse-drawn carriages glistening in the noonday sun. Like a butterfly, my attention flitted from one bright scene to another. Sol's placid face seemed to indicate his thoughts were equally unfocused until he spoke.

His words brought a knowing smile to my face. "So where is it written," he said with resignation, "that I should teach them how to give charity with dignity?"

VISITING SERENDIPITY

C harles Larson stared at the telephone he had just hung up, as though by concentrating on the squat black instrument he could undo the conversation he had just terminated. He tapped the serrated edge of two theater tickets against the top of his junior executive desk. The tickets announced the performance that evening at the Metropolitan Opera of Verdi's *Otello* with Placido Domingo in the leading role. The telephone remained mute, and he swiveled around in his sturdy but unpretentious desk chair to stare out the single window of his office. Instead of the Manhattan skyline, it looked out on the dull red brick of an old Wall Street office building across the street. He sat very still counting bricks.

Brenda had just broken their date. Now he had two very expensive tickets, retained a great desire to hear the performance, and was more than a little irritated. He frowned. What was it about Brenda that appealed to him? She had a wonderfully curved body, which he had taken full advantage of on more than a few occasions, but there was always something missing. She never liked to have him kiss her. He concluded that perhaps he wasn't the greatest kisser in the world, even though no woman in his life up until now had complained.

She was just so *New York*. There was something about her un-cluttered, if narrow, eastern sophistication, complete with a Miss Porter's education and her parents' Beekman Place apartment, which appealed to his midwestern soul. His mother didn't like her, and at the moment, he wasn't sure he did either. He had sensed in the past weeks that he was going to be dumped. He hated that.

Kristin Pendarvis leaned against his door and spoke to the top of his blond head beyond the back of the chair. "Churly? You with us this morning, or in Never Never Land?"

Instead of calling him Charley, like the rest of the attorneys at Helfland and Hartman, Kris always referred to him either as Churly or Churls to his face. Behind her back, he had dubbed her *Christ*in. They were both junior litigators in the firm, where he helped represent the more mainline corporate business and she was an advocate for many environmental groups, pets of one of the senior partners. Charley and Kris were always clashing over the availability of secretaries and legal assistants' time, office space, or anything else that was at hand. She called him a fascist pig, and he called her Pendarvis the Red. He sneered at her Harvard Law School background, and she retaliated with remarks about Stanford being a glorified A&M. He swiveled back around to face her, instantly on the alert.

"What's the prob'?" She stared at him through perfectly round horn-rimmed glasses, which overpowered a small heart-shaped face. Her honey-colored hair hung in waves halfway down the back of the oversized black jacket she wore. Her one vanity seemed to be great legs, which she always showed off with the briefest of skirts tempered only by sensible mid-heel pumps.

"My date just canceled."

"Poor baby," she said in mock sympathy.

"And I have two tickets to hear Domingo in *Otello* tonight."

Her interest was immediate and genuine. "You're kidding! My roommate and I did everything but kill to get a ticket. You must have bribed somebody or have friends in higher places than I suspected."

"Both," he said.

"Well, I'll be more than glad to take them off your hands, including the scalper's cut."

He tossed one of the tickets across the desk to her. "Here, just pay me the ticket price, and your roommate is out of luck. I wouldn't miss this."

"Thanks, and we're due at a staff conference in case you've forgotten. I'll grab my purse and give you a check."

The younger staff spent these meetings in an adversarial mode, vying for support for their own cases. He had to admit he rather enjoyed these sparring matches. Kristin was always his most formidable opponent, but he usually got most of what he wanted. In private, he gloated at his success in besting his rivals from the prestigious eastern law schools. Regardless of his dismay earlier in the morning, he achieved what he wanted at the meeting and felt in an expansive mood, not enough to refuse the check Kris proffered, but enough to say, "We might as well grab a drink and something to eat before the performance, since we're sitting together. I'll meet you at the elevator about five thirty. That okay?"

Good God, what had come over him, he thought. He hated this woman. Now he had committed himself to an entire evening in her company. He thought she blanched. Her eyes were nearly as large as the glasses she wore.

"Well, sure. Yeah. Fine," was all she managed to say. At the door, she looked back. "Dutch, of course."

He was grateful to her for underscoring that this was not, definitely not, a date.

At five thirty, Charley ensconced himself in the hall outside the elevator where he could watch the mahogany double doors to the office suite. He settled his shoulders firmly against the wall and prepared for the inevitable wait whenever he had a date. Engagement, he reminded himself—well, whenever he did anything with a woman. He patted the breast pocket of his Harris Tweed jacket to be sure the ticket was there and then dug his hands deep in the pockets of his chinos. He began a meticulous investigation of the cut brass letters announcing the style of the firm.

"Ready?"

Kris had come from the ladies room down the hall. Charley jumped and turned in surprise. She was dressed exactly as she had been all day, except the glasses were gone and probably replaced by contact lenses. Her eyes were an arresting turquoise.

"Had to put on the contacts. I can't wear them all day. I've tried and tried, and I just have too many allergies, but I can get away with the soft ones for an evening."

"Nice," he remarked, but it sounded earnest rather than cynical.

She gave him a sour look. "Peripheral vision, Churls, not flirtation. Where shall we eat?"

They decided on a small, busy restaurant not far from Lincoln Center, took the subway from Wall Street to Columbus Circle, and walked the rest of the way. The restaurant was old New York Italian, complete with dark woodwork, red-and-white–checkered tablecloths reminiscent more of the '50s than the '90s, raffia-wrapped bottles, and the smells of boiling flour paste, garlic, and wine. She ordered capellini pomodoro, and he splurged on the tortellini with pesto, not thinking about garlic until too late. But then it didn't matter anyway. They both ordered red wine and dived into the garlic bread.

"So you like opera," she said, making it sound at once like a question and a statement.

"Love it. Grew up on the Saturday afternoon Met performances on the radio," he said.

"Where was that?"

"Minneapolis."

"Ooooh, cold." She gave a mock shiver

"You get used to it. And Minneapolis is a great town, lots to do and see. Of course, it's not New York."

"But you miss it sometimes," she said with the same inflection she used with her first question.

"I love New York," he said defensively

"So do I, but I don't know if I want to live here all my life."

"Where did you grow up, Boston?" he changed the subject.

"God, no. A little town south of Cleveland."

"But you went to prep school someplace. I've heard you mention it."

"I went to prep school right in Hudson. My dad taught there. I wanted to go to Kenyon, which was just down the road, but I didn't get the kind of scholarship I needed. It was cheaper to go to Ohio State for undergrad, so I did. I did really well on the LSATs, but I've always thought I wouldn't have made it to Harvard except that I was a woman." She tipped her glass at him. "Three cheers for good old affirmative action."

He stared at her as she sardonically drank the small toast. But she was a really good lawyer. He was amazed she should entertain any doubts about that.

"But weren't you a preppy, too? You look the part." Her eyes flicked quickly over his jacket, shirt, and tie.

He wasn't sure just what that meant. "Not me. Whittier High in South Minneapolis, class of eighy-three. My mother taught there," he said.

"Oh," she said with a pert glance, "what did she teach?"

"English."

"My Dad taught history. What did yours do?"

112

"He was a heat and air contractor." The answer came from years of practice. His dad was exactly that, working by himself, building over the years a small but loyal clientele of people who trusted him to keep their homes and their rental property warm in the Minnesota winters, and installing air conditioners in small businesses that wanted customers to stay cool in the few hot days of July or August. He did work "on contract" for them, verbally, but contractor sounded better. Charley winced at his own snobbery.

"Did your mom work?" he asked.

"Nope. Housewife, or homemaker as they are called. She does lovely sewing, a talent I did not inherit, and she sometimes did custom knitting for a local shop."

"Lucky you," he said.

"Oh?"

"To have her home all the time."

"Yes," she hesitated and then definitively, "Yes."

"And you'd be bored to death doing that."

"Sometimes, I'm sure I would. And I'm sure she was, too." She glanced at her watch. "Oh God, look at the time!" They bolted the last of their pasta, decided on coffee at intermission, and he hastily left money for dinner and the tip on the table.

"Pay me later," he said as she rummaged in her purse. He took her by the elbow, and they sprinted for the light and Lincoln Center.

Their seats were not excellent, but very good. He was familiar with the Metropolitan Opera House and knew you could hear well everywhere in the magnificent auditorium. He could see quite well but wondered if the much shorter Kris would have a decent view of the stage. He glanced over. She was struggling out of the jacket, and he reached to help her, accidentally tangling his watch in a long, silky strand of hair. She giggled. He extricated the band from the blond filament and thought, my God, the woman has breasts, and rather fine-shaped ones at that. He was relieved when the lights dimmed and the overture began. The house was in almost total darkness, but her legs, crossed at the knee in nude stockings, seemed to reflect the only available light.

He concentrated on the stage. The opera was masterful.

Following the final curtain call, they made their way through the crowd and onto the street, discussing in detail what they had seen and heard. Charley was surprised both at Kris's depth of knowledge and at her enthusiasm, which he had supposed was solely focused on the liberal causes she defended.

A misty rain was falling, not enough to warrant an umbrella but enough to turn the streets to black patent leather, exaggerating the rasp of tires on the pavement and reflecting the colors of neon signs in wavy mirages. When they reached the subway stop at Columbus Circle, she turned and held out her hand. "Thanks, Churls. I really enjoyed that."

He wondered if "that" included him. "Hey, don't you want to grab a cab?"

"No. I'll take the subway. I live just across the park in the East Seventies."

"Pricey neighborhood."

"Tiny apartment with two of us squeezed in. You live in Tribeca, don't you?"

"Yeah," he was slightly miffed she knew where his apartment was and he had never thought about where she lived. He wondered if the roommate was male or female.

"Do you like it?" she asked.

"Yeah, it's a fun area."

She frowned off into the distance. "Our lease comes up soon, and I've wondered if we couldn't find something cheaper with a little more room."

"Come down and see my place sometime, and I'll show you the neighborhood." To his ears, it sounded like a cross between Mae West and an offer to view etchings.

"Sure," was all she said and started to back away.

Perhaps he only imagined the skeptical look. In an effort to put the evening back on a casual basis, he took her by the elbow. "Wait. I'll see you to your door. But first, I have this overpowering urge," he said with mock drama.

This time the skeptical look was there.

"Hot fudge."

"What?"

"The urge for a hot fudge sundae, and as you know, Schrafft's is the only place. Now, I could have asked you to join me in a drink at the Oak Bar, but my midwestern heart longs for hot fudge, and that dish, like real hamburgers, can only be truly enjoyed with another midwesterner."

She laughed at his silliness. "You're out of luck. It's closed at this hour. You'll have to indulge your obsession another day."

"Wait. I know a place that's bound to have hot fudge, and if not exactly on your way, it is at least on your side of town."

Before she could gather herself enough to protest, he had hailed a cab going east and hustled her into the back seat.

"Serendipity," he said to the cabby, "Lex and Sixty-First."

Since he had given her no choice, she took refuge in resignation. "Okay, I'll have a Coke or something."

At the restaurant, she took one look at the menu of desserts and ordered hot fudge.

They resumed their critique of the opera until their order came. He watched as she carefully set the cherry aside to eat later and pushed at the whipped cream until she could fill the spoon with just the right combination of vanilla ice cream, chocolate, and topping. He had already devoured the cherry and was savoring the hot-cold chocolate-vanilla taste. He thought sundaes might be the most sensuous eating experience of all.

"If you're a good girl and eat all of your sundae, I'll buy you a stuffed doll to take home," he said, referring to the numerous anatomically correct male dolls the restaurant was famous for displaying.

She gave him a withering look and returned the conversation to New York housing.

"You might like Tribeca," he said, "but I have to say, for two women, your neighborhood couldn't be better. You know, safe."

She stared thoughtfully into the distance and turned her spoon over to lick the inside. "True," she said. "I walk almost everywhere whenever I want to. Of course, it's still the city, and I don't think I'm foolish about it."

She had not corrected the reference to two women.

"So what about your roommate?"

"Well, that's part of the problem. I think she's either going to get married or move in with this guy." She hesitated, and for some reason Charley found himself holding his breath. "And I'm not sure I'm staying."

"In New York?"

She nodded. "I'm thinking about going home."

"But what about your job?" He dropped the spoon on the table-top with a clatter.

"What about it?"

He shrugged and took another bite of sundae. "I don't know. I guess I had you pegged as one of those fiercely ambitious guys at the firm who would sacrifice anything to make it to senior partner status with H&H."

"Funny," she said with mock sincerity, "That's just what I thought of you."

He did not rise to the bait but began scraping melted ice cream and the remnants of chocolate from the bottom of the fluted sundae dish with serious intent.

"Look," she said, following his mood, "I think I'm stuck. Helfland has me pegged as the bright, able do-gooder in the firm. It's not that I don't believe in what I'm doing. I do. And for the most part, I like my clients and the people I work with. Most of all, I'm proud of H&H for spending the time and the money to do something for this old world other than make bazillions of dollars on corporate clients. I know it's not easy for them." She studied the bottom of her own sundae dish, and he did not interrupt. "I just wonder if I want to spend the rest of my life in the big city doing essentially what I'm doing now, but maybe with a larger salary and an office with a window that looks out on something."

He gave her an ironic glance. "So what do you want to do? Go back to the Midwest someplace and have babies while practicing with the local Legal Services or ACLU?"

"Sometimes." The look in her turquoise eyes was dead serious. Then she looked away at the floor and blushed at her confession.

Charles had a panicky feeling that perhaps she was afraid she had just handed him a weapon to hold over her head in the competitive atmosphere of the junior associates at the firm. He leaned forward seriously, pushing the dish aside and crossing his arms on the tabletop. The tweed of his old sport coat was rough beneath his fingers.

"Look, if you're serious, you really ought to look into someplace like Minneapolis." He could hear the enthusiasm in his own voice.

She looked back at him in surprise.

"I'm serious. I clerked in the summer with a firm there that really isn't all that different, except in scale, from H&H. And the atmosphere was a lot more, well, collegial. If you really want to get out of New York, there have to be a lot of firms out there willing to pay nicely for your experience. And God knows the pace of life is better, to say nothing of prices."

He was astounded to hear himself say this. He was always defending to his folks the advantages of New York over such an argument as he had just made to Kris. Oh well, he thought, that's the advocate in me. Pick a side and make a good case. But he was aware of a sudden pang of longing for the blue, gold, and green of Minnesota summers. He smiled. Maybe he sometimes even missed the January deep freeze. He glanced out the window. The desultory rain continued to cloak Manhattan.

He was aware she was still staring at him with a thoughtful expression. "Well," she reached for her purse, "I have to go—early day tomorrow."

He paid the check, and they walked out into the still-misting city.

"Shall we get a cab, or do you want to hoof it?" he asked.

"Let's walk."

He wanted to tuck her arm under his but settled for a companionable distance between them.

They walked up Lexington Avenue to Seventy-Seventh, where she turned a half block east and stopped before the steps to a nondescript glass door of the apartment building. They had not spoken or touched, except for their elbows occasionally brushing. She mounted the first step and turned to face him. The step brought her face to just below his chin.

"Thanks again, Churls. And thanks for listening to me whine."

He didn't smile or answer but leaned forward to brush her lips with his in the merest of kisses.

She stood perfectly still with her eyes closed. "Mmmm." The utterance was speculative.

He pulled her close and kissed her more deeply.

Again her response was, "Mmmm," this time with a note of satisfaction.

He didn't know what to do and didn't want to move. She opened her eyes, gave him a straight look, and took his face in her hands, returning his kisses with one of her own. Then she stepped back.

"Good night, Charley. See you tomorrow," she said and was in the door before he moved.

He began to walk back toward Lex and the subway. He felt a little light headed, the taste of her still in his mouth. The words of that ridiculous song from *My Fair Lady* that the sappy tenor Freddy

Eynsford-Hill sang occurred to him. He groaned and said, "Oh shit," disturbing the concentration of the only other person on the sidewalk, a rather seedy-looking drunk passing him.

When Charles got to the corner, he stopped and shook his head, acknowledging to himself that he was glad Kris was not leaving the next morning for points west and that he would see her at the office as usual. Then he laughed. Mother would really like that girl.

BIOGRAPHY

Janet Taliaferro lives in Leesburg, Virginia in winter and summers in Northern Wisconsin. She holds a BA from Southern Methodist University in Comparative Literature and an MA in Creative Studies from the University of Central Oklahoma where she received the Geoffrey Bocca Memorial Award for excellence, awarded to a graduating Master's Degree candidate.

Her novel, A Sky for Arcadia, was one of eight finalists in the Oklahoma Center for the Book Awards for fiction in 2001. A second novel, Virgin Hall, was published in 2011. Her poetry has appeared in numerous small magazines and anthologies well as on the Atticus Review website and Robin Chapman's poetry blog.

She is a member of the Wisconsin Fellowship of Poets.